'I'm Daffy and I'm 13.
"Daffy by name, daft by nature," Mum says.

'This is the story of a special summer down at
the creek and what happened when we met the
kids.
We loved sailing and swimming; they were in
wheelchairs.

'It was special for me too.
It was the summer I nearly split up with Andy.
And Podge, my best friend, was transformed
into a "young lady".
And I became a sort of heroine . . .

'Let me tell you how it all began . . .'

Daffy is the funny, imaginative heroine of
Wheelchair Summer.
She definitely has a mind of her own. And she
wants to be a writer.

Daffy is always asking questions – about
herself, about other people, and about God too.
It is through what happens during this special
summer that she begins to find some of the
answers.

Wheelchair Summer

Dorothy Oxley

HAMILTON
COLLEGE

A LION PAPERBACK

Copyright © 1982 Dorothy Oxley

Published by
Lion Publishing
Icknield Way, Tring, Herts, England
ISBN 0 85648 330 3

Albatross Books
PO Box 320, Sutherland, NSW 2232, Australia
ISBN 0 86760 371 2

First edition 1982

Illustrations by Evelyn Bartlett
Cover photograph: Arthur Sidey
All rights reserved

Printed and bound in Great Britain by
Collins, Glasgow

Contents

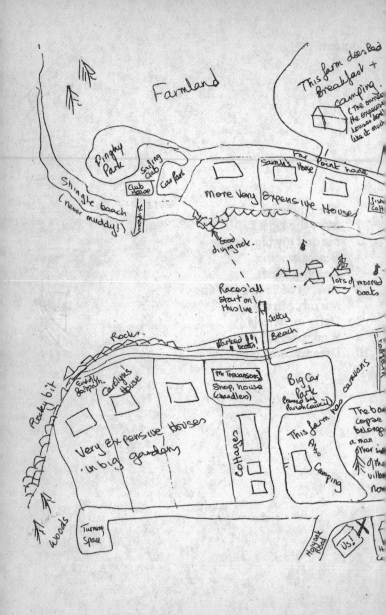

Farmland

This farm does Bad Breakfast + camping. (The owner of the expensive houses don't like it much)

Dinghy Park

Sailing Club

Club House

Car Park

Shingle beach (never muddy!)

Far Point house

Sarah's House

More Very Expensive Houses

Jish's cott—

Good diving rock.

lots of motored boats

Races all start on this line

Jetty

Beach

Rocks

Marked boats

Rocky bit

Suzi's Boatpath

Carolyn's House

Very Expensive Houses in big gardens

Mr Trevarson's Shop, house (chandler)

Cottages

Big Car Park (owned by Parish Council)

This farm has caravans

This farm has caravans

The bar coppice belongs to a man prior self—of the villa—Nov.

Also Camping

Woods

Turning Space

Holywak Road

Us.

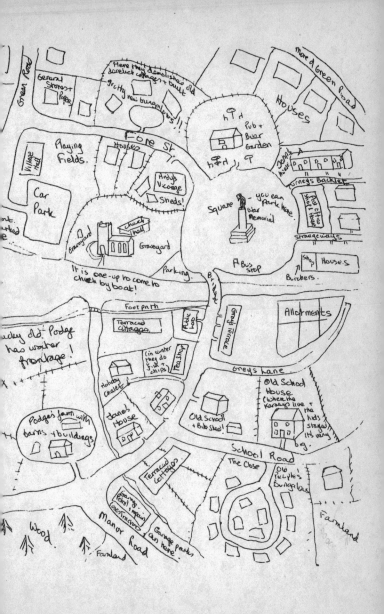

CHAPTER 1

THE CHALLENGE

It's a funny thing with nicknames. Take Podge and me, for instance. Now Podge is definitely fat. Mum says she needs to lose at least a stone, but I don't suppose she ever will, because her whole family's fat and they just *live* on sweets, home-made cakes and stodgy things. But Podge is fun, she's nice, and she doesn't mind her nickname at all when friends use it. I'm the same — my nickname is Daffy because I like clowning around and doing crazy things. Even Mum and Dad call me Daffy most of the time, and I'm rather proud of it.

But I knew how Podge felt when Sarah Henderson called her Podge. Because then it was different — Sarah meant it as an insult. She's pretty and her Dad's well off, which makes her think she can queen it over everyone, especially as she's older than us.

'Podge can never have a dinghy,' she sneered, tying her own Topper up at the jetty. 'She'd not fit in anything smaller than the QE2. And everyone knows Daffy's dad couldn't afford to buy her a boat.'

The other Corsairs giggled and sneered at us too. With the exception of Carolyn, who is usually awful anyway, they aren't too bad at school, because they're all in different forms, but in the summer they come together under Her Majesty Queen Sarah and turn beastly. Just because they're the only kids in the creek with their own sailing dinghies. Apart from Sarah's Topper, Tim and Luke have Toppers too, Liz and her sister Jenny share an old Tutor 10, Carolyn and her brother Peter have a Mirror and even little Jason, who's only nine, has an Optimist.

Carolyn is Sarah's particular crony, and they back each other up in nastiness. She smiled at us.

'Why don't you kids go away and play mud pies?' she suggested sweetly. 'Jetties are for sailors – you don't belong here.'

I smiled sweetly too.

'Oh,' I said. 'We're just waiting to make sure you tie up properly this time.'

That made her angry. She flushed and looked as though she wanted to hit me, because she remembered jolly well how once she'd only secured her Mirror with a half-hitch and I'd swum out and brought it back after it had drifted away.

You see, the silly thing is, for all snooty Sarah's sarcasm, both Podge and I can sail. We crew for Mr and Mrs Mason, me with him, and Podge with her. They both have Enterprise dinghies and we race every Sunday afternoon. Podge is very good on the helm too. But her dad doesn't see she needs her own boat, not when she can sail with Mrs Mason. Her dad is a farmer and there's always something he reckons he needs money for on the farm. And my Dad has a shop in Truro which just about keeps us, so he certainly can't afford a dinghy for me.

'Bet one of us wins a cup in the Regatta,' Luke said, and I wondered briefly if the Masons would let us borrow one of their Enterprises. I was just about to say something when Podge said suddenly:

'Bet *we* win a cup in the Regatta.'

'You and Daffy?' Sarah sneered. 'They don't give

cups for being fattest or daftest.'

I didn't know what Podge was planning but I followed her lead anyway.

'Bet one of us or both of us wins cups,' I agreed.

The Corsairs all laughed, but Mr Trevanson, who keeps the boat store and owns the jetty, had heard us.

'The Regatta cups go to outsiders too often' he said. 'I'll give any kid who lives in or around Peveran a good prize as well as any cup they win. It doesn't have to be a sailing cup.'

'Thanks,' Sarah acknowledged, almost as if she knew she'd already won it. I glared at her, but smiled at Mr Trevanson.

'That's super of you,' I began, but Peter interrupted.

'What are there cups for, apart from sailing?' he asked, with a suspicious look at Podge. 'It's always just been sailing before.'

Mr Trevanson was one of the organizing committee, so he knew all the details.

'It's bigger and better this year,' he promised. 'There's swimming, rowing, diving, crazy water sports and a raft race.'

'Great!' I yelled. 'Put me down for swimming, water sports and the raft race.'

'Me for swimming, rowing and diving,' Podge said just as quickly, and I knew a lot of the wind had been taken out of the Corsairs' sails. They were all looking pretty cross. Not one of them can swim as well as Podge and me. Podge is so strong, she's a fantastic oarswoman and despite her flab she's a good diver too, because she's not in the least bit scared. And as it'd be beneath Corsair dignity to enter silly water sports or raft races, none of them could challenge me there. I *like* making a fool of myself – it's part of my crazy image.

'We'll all enter the proper sailing races,' Carolyn

said, looking down her nose. 'Those other things don't count.'

'A bet's a bet and a cup's a cup,' Mr Trevanson argued. Then he reached into his pocket and pulled out some entry forms, so we could fill them in there and then. We were all busy scribbling when Dave Kersey came up, so I told him what the competitions were and asked if he was entering any. He listened eagerly, and grinned.

'Rowing, swimming and that diving – is it into, or under?'

'Into,' Mr Trevanson explained. 'We're rigging a three-metre board over where it's really deep at high tide.'

I grabbed another form.

'I'll fill it in for you, Dave,' I offered. 'You're all fishy.'

He'd been out fishing with his Dad and they clean the guts out before they come ashore. That way, they just fall on the water and the gulls have them. But it wasn't why I filled in the form really. Dave's retarded. He's bright enough with boats, but he can't read or write.

The Corsairs edged away from him, making bad-smell expressions, and finished their forms in Mr Trevanson's shop.

'Nasty snobs,' Podge growled, and she hardly ever says a bad word about anybody. Dave only grinned.

'Mackerel guts do pong some,' he admitted cheerfully. 'I'll wash 'em off.'

Then he dived off the end of the jetty without a ripple, and swam across the creek. I finished my form and his, and looked at Podge. We hadn't got our swimming costumes or towels, because we'd only just finished our Saturday morning job delivering Podge's

Mum's eggs and veg to the camp site. But it was hot, and our T-shirts and shorts would soon dry.

'Mum won't let me swim for two hours after lunch,' I said, and Podge nodded. Hers was the same. We both had packed lunches with us, so nobody would actually know if we disobeyed, but it wasn't just a silly rule. You can get cramp if you swim while you are still trying to digest.

I dumped my lunch on the jetty and dived in. Podge followed. Not even the Corsairs would be rotten enough to pinch our grub. I saw people getting a big yacht ready to sail, and decided to play my favourite game of swimming up unnoticed to touch the boat. I pretended I was a saboteur — if they saw me and waved or something, I'd been shot and had to swim ashore, but if I touched the boat unseen it was counted as blown up and I could move on to my next target. Sarah claims only idiots still play pretend games when they're thirteen, but it's fun.

Podge joined Dave on the Point. There's a good rock for diving off — it's too high for me, about ten feet. They were both going off it without a care in the world. I couldn't decide which of them was best, but they made it very easy for me to sneak up on the yacht. In between working, her crew were too busy watching the diving to notice me. I heard one, a teenage boy, say 'They're better than anyone in our school,' and thought how pleased Podge would be when I told her. Then I decided on a more difficult target, and, using moored boats as cover, swam to intercept Mr Kersey who was rowing out to his boat again. If you can hitch a ride behind a rowing boat and not be noticed, that's *really* stealthy swimming!

I didn't quite make it, though I did the last bit underwater. I was spotted as I surfaced. Mr Kersey waved to me.

'Ahoy, Daffy!' he called. 'Seen my son?'

'Diving off the rocks with Podge,' I explained. 'They've both entered the diving in the Regatta.'

'Good,' Mr Kersey approved. He and his wife are both teachers, and I think it really knocked them sideways when Dave turned out to be retarded. Luckily, though, they're not just brainy people who can't *do* things. Mr Kersey's a really keen boatman who knows his tides and engines and can build or repair any old boat. He's taught Dave to be a good fisherman, good enough to earn some sort of living fishing when he leaves his Special School. And he's always pleased when Dave plays with us kids and joins in things locally.

I was about to swim away then, as per my rules, but Mr Kersey called me again.

'Daffy,' he said, 'you know most of the local kids. Do you think you could organize a rota of young volunteers to help with three severely handicapped children we've got coming to stay? It'll be from Sunday afternoon for two weeks — just generally helping and playing with them. They're all in wheelchairs and two have serious speech defects. None can use their hands much.'

'Poor kids!' I exclaimed. I'd help, of course, and Podge would jump at the chance, because she wants to be a hydrotherapist anyway (that is, when she's not wanting to run a sailing school). I could probably also persuade Jane, who's painfully shy but kind in a rather drippy way. As for boys, there was my friend Andy, the vicar's son, who'd been ill and wasn't yet allowed to anything energetic, not even sailing, which was annoying him. And maybe his friend John. But I didn't hold out much hope for the Corsairs; with the Regatta two weeks away, they'd be sailing every possible minute. Anyway, I didn't think either Sarah or Carolyn would want to help and anything *they* say, *goes*.

'OK, Mr Kersey,' I promised. 'I'll try. What if we all turn up on Sunday to meet the kids?'

'Come for Sunday tea,' he agreed. 'Four p.m. – OK?'

Luckily, it was. Normally Podge and I would be racing with the Masons, but this weekend they were on holiday.

'Fine,' I confirmed.

'Want some mackerel for your mums, you and Podge?'

'Yes, please,' I said eagerly. When you're so poor that even the church mice take up collections for you, you never turn down anything free. Mr Kersey pulled six fish from somewhere, shoved them in a plastic bag, tied the end and threw it to me. Pretending it was a case full of top-secret plans, I clutched it on top of my stomach and did lifesaver's backstroke all the way to the jetty.

Dave had seen his dad and was swimming to join him. Podge soon joined me, and I shared out the fish. Then we had our lunches. Typically, mine was a chunk of cheese, a little plastic box of salad with a chopped hard-boiled egg, an apple and a bottle of pop. Podge had an enormous pasty, a packet of crisps, a great wedge of heavy cake and a small bar of chocolate. And she ate the lot!

'I'm a growing girl,' she said cheerfully, and I thought, yeah, widthways. But I didn't say it because, after all, she's my friend. Instead, I told her about the handicapped kids and she was thrilled, as I'd expected. Then the Corsairs came back, and though Liz looked interested, and I think even Sarah might have been persuadable, Carolyn said firmly:

'Don't be silly, we haven't got time to play nurse-maids.'

She's so nasty sometimes, I wonder if she only thinks she can stay on top by putting everyone else down.

'Oh, well,' I said. 'If you need that much practice to win anything in the Regatta, you'd better get it.'

I can be pretty nasty too. Carolyn and I glared at each other for a minute, then she turned her back on me. Sarah, looking a bit embarrassed, gave her Corsairs their orders and they all set sail.

Podge and I decided to take the mackerel home, before they went off, then she'd see Jane while I saw Andy. It was no good approaching any of the other kids. The Guides and Scouts all had camps that fortnight, the older kids mostly had holiday jobs and some were at the Youth Camp. Most of the rest would be up to their necks in Carnival or Regatta preparations or were just the kind of kids you knew wouldn't be interested anyway.

Podge's farm is quite near our house, so we walked together, swinging our bags and singing. I sing folk songs with Andy sometimes, but Podge has a voice like a buzz-saw gone wrong. Luckily that doesn't matter when you're singing daft songs, and we were. We didn't shut up until she turned into her lane.

'See you teatime!' I yelled. We took turns in going to tea at each other's houses. Then I went on singing home.

Mum was pleased with the mackerel, and pleased we were going to help Mr Kersey with the children. She'd heard about them at the Women's Institute. Apparently they were supposed to have been going to a holiday home for disabled kids, but it had been damaged by fire. At the last moment arrangements were made to take some of them in Red Cross House in Truro, and the Kerseys had volunteered to take the last three. The WI was going to give them a party and puppet show one day and help Mrs Kersey by cooking cakes, pies and things for them (you can't beat the WI at cooking!).

'You'll enjoy yourselves too,' Mum promised. 'The Kerseys have hired a minibus to take the kids, and helpers, to interesting places.'

That was a bonus I hadn't thought of. In fact, I hadn't really thought what we would be doing with the kids. The only disabled kids I'd met were at the swimming-pool, at the Tadpole Club special sessions, where Podge and I are water helpers. That's on Tuesday lunchtimes, during term. But now I began to think of what we could do. Podge and I could teach swimming. We could all make sandcastles. Jane rides — perhaps we could get them riding somehow, I knew they did riding for the disabled at Moor Farm stables near St Agnes. Andy is a mad keen naturalist and photographer. He could teach them to identify birds, animals and flowers. I could tell stories, and even if they couldn't help me make a raft, they could watch.

Mum interrupted my thoughts by handing over a box, with something rustling inside.

'Mole,' she explained. 'Dandy caught it this morning. I thought Andy might like it. It'll need a bit of care and attention before it can be safely released.' (Dandy is one of our four cats, and a terrific hunter.)

The poor little thing's right shovel forepaw was only hanging by a thread, but it seemed more angry than shocked, which was a good sign. It's when they go very quiet and dull-eyed that they're likely to die on you. I guessed Andy would treat its injury, give it a bit of hospital time in his bedroom, then fill one of his glass-sided tea-chest observatories with earth and see if he could get any photos of it tunnelling. He'd feed it on yellowjackets and other garden grubs — not worms, because he feels sorry for worms and they're useful anyway.

'He'll love it,' I said, and after reminding Mum that Podge was coming to tea, I set off for Andy's. On the way through the village, I found a heat-killed worm on the road and popped it in the box in case the mole might fancy a roast dinner by way of variety. He wasn't enthusiastic.

Andy was in the churchyard, half hidden behind a tombstone with his lens fixed on an owl in one of the trees. It was a tawny owl, half asleep, being mobbed by some indignant small birds. My arrival didn't bother them, but shortly after I'd come, the owl decided he'd had enough and launched himself into the air, followed by his cursing tormentors.

Andy stopped his camera. (Actually, it's not his, he and his mate John own it jointly; they earned the money by selling still pictures to magazines and papers.) Andy's super on natural history and wants to work for someone like David Attenborough, while John fancies being a television news cameraman.

'Should be a good bit of film,' Andy exulted. He still looked a bit washed out (Mum says meningitis lays you low for ages) but happy. I gave him the mole, and he was delighted. He said he'd evict a now recovered cat-caught grass snake from his vivarium and put the mole in that.

I asked him about helping with the handicapped kids, and after he'd thought for a minute, he said he could come on quite a few days and maybe John would come too, especially if they could both bring their cameras. John was off at the beach photographing wind-surfers practising for the Nationals, but he'd be calling in during the evening and Andy promised to ask him then.

Andy's mum enthused about the mole when we took him to the vicarage. I think she was particularly pleased because his arrival meant the grass snake would be going and she doesn't like snakes, even harmless ones. She gave us both milkshakes, and we talked about the handicapped children.

'I've been looking through the old costumes from the days when I ran a dancing school,' she said. 'It occurred to me the children could take part in the carnival, either on a float or in the fancy dress.' (Although the Regatta is on most of the morning and afternoon, from about 5 p.m. we have a carnival parade, and after that, sports, a barbecue and open air folk dancing. It's a super day!)

'We could dress up too, and push their wheelchairs,' I agreed.

Andy shuddered. 'I'm not dressing up in Mum's old gear,' he snorted, then grinned, and took up a silly pose.

'Andrew MacKay, Sugar Plum Fairy,' he said. I giggled, and his Mum laughed.

'Oh, we'll find something suitable for boys,' she promised. 'Mr Kersey thinks it's a good idea, anyway.'

So did I — I love dressing up. I would have liked to stop and chat a bit, but I had to get home, so I thanked Mrs MacKay for the milk shake and reminded Andy that we were supposed to meet at Mr Kersey's at 4 p.m. the next day.

His Mum said something hopeful about the interesting things Junior Church were doing on Sunday mornings, but I didn't take the hint. Catch me shut up indoors on a summer Sunday? Added to which, most of the Corsairs were packed off to church by their parents and Sarah even sang in the choir. I thought it was better to be a pagan than a hypocrite, though I'm not exactly a pagan because I believe in a loving God and pray to him, and I must admit I sometimes get this uncomfortable feeling when someone mentions Jesus. Like there's something I ought to know.

(By the way – and *this is important* – when I wrote the above bit that was how I was feeling *then*. I feel different now, but you'll have to read on to find out how and why.)

Podge had already arrived when I got home. She said Jane would love to help with the kids. What's more, her aunt thoroughly approved. Jane's aunt can be a bit stuffy sometimes, but she's not a bad old bird really. After all, I suppose the old girl – she was much older than Jane's dad – must have found it hard suddenly lumbered with an orphaned toddler when she was happily nursing the heathen somewhere (she was a missionary nurse). But she's been a real Mum to Jane.

Over tea, I talked about rafts and Podge just ate. Mum's bun supply rapidly diminished, but she didn't mind. Podge only stopped chewing long enough to say her dad had some old fertilizer drums I could use. I wanted to go back with her and get started, but Mum said no. She needed me to help her make some cakes for the Kersey's tea on Sunday. I didn't really mind. I like cooking, and I could always plan out a raft as I creamed the sugar and margarine.

CHAPTER 2

MEET THE KIDS

Sunday morning was beastly and wet. Rotten weather for the poor kids to arrive in, I thought. I spent the morning helping to ice the cakes we'd made, then earned a bit of extra pocket money polishing the lino and furniture in two rooms. Andy's always tied up with Junior Church on Sunday mornings, and Podge goes in to practise diving and swimming at Truro Swimming Club, so I'm naturally stuck on my own.

It was still raining at lunchtime so I did some writing. I know I've got to keep in practice, if I'm to be a famous author some day!

By 3.30 p.m. the rain had cleared. John and Andy arrived fresh from a photographic expedition in the copse, then we went to collect Podge and all went in convoy to Jane's, and got caught for a moment's polite conversation by her aunt. It sounds stupid, but we needed to turn up at the Kerseys' in a bunch. We were all scared and somehow there was safety in numbers.

'What if they don't like us?' Jane said nervously.

'Oh, they'll love us,' I joked. 'We're all such beautiful, charming, talented people.' But inside, I felt horribly inadequate. Especially about the speech defect bit – what if we couldn't understand them?

'I bet they're wondering what *we're* like,' Andy said, and grinned at me. 'Poor things – little do they know!'

Podge asked how old they were. I wasn't sure, but I thought, little kids.

Actually, Anna was nine, Burt was eleven and Stella was thirteen. And when we first saw them, we felt the smiles freeze on our faces. None of us had seen children so badly handicapped before in our lives. Anna had a pretty face, but she just slumped in her junior wheelchair, with straps holding her in, and dribbled a bit too. She managed a smile, but couldn't even hold her head up properly, and her arms and legs were just limp. She looked like a big rag doll with half the stuffing taken out. Burt was all twisted, every bit of him jerking crazily all the time, even the muscles of his face so he looked as if he were making silly expressions when actually the poor kid was trying hard to smile. Stella was the least handicapped – at least she was able to sit up straight and didn't shake about. But she wasn't able to move her limbs, except perhaps a flicker in her shoulders.

'Hello,' she said, and her words were clear. 'I'm Stella.'

Her greeting broke the ice and we all unfroze and started to introduce ourselves. Burt and Anna made noises which we guessed were welcoming and friendly, even though Anna's were just tiny, strangled sounds which might have been 'Hi'. We did most of the talking, about the things that we liked best and wanted to show them; the Kerseys got a few words in about their plans for the fortnight, and Dave joined us. He was totally at ease with the kids and seemed to understand everything Burt and Anna said, so we let him translate.

Tea was a laugh, but a bit messy because the kids had to be fed by us and we weren't very good at it. Burt's spasming arm sent a great blob of trifle flying out of a spoon Andy held and into his face, like something out of an old slapstick movie. I fed Stella. She had had polio. I didn't think anyone did now but I learned later that her parents hadn't believed in vaccination, then when she got it they'd virtually abandoned her in hospital. I think we got as much food *on* ourselves as *in* ourselves. Jane started feeding Anna and was doing very well, then John decided to feed Podge, just for a giggle and so the kids wouldn't feel silly at having to be fed, while we could feed ourselves. They mucked about so much that even Jane giggled and a bit of peach slid down the front of Anna's dress too, which made her pale little face achieve quite a lovely smile.

Mr Kersey grinned at us all.

'I can see you kids are going to get on like a house on fire,' he said. 'Though how we grown-ups will survive is open to doubt!'

Then, while we had some food ourselves, he outlined some of his plans for the fortnight.

'Tomorrow, if it's fine,' he said, 'we'll have a quick look at Truro, take the ferry to Falmouth, have a picnic lunch on the ferry, look round Falmouth then catch the ferry back. Other things I've got planned are a trip to Perranporth beach, a sailing outing of some kind, the Seal Sanctuary, the show at the Aero Park and maybe the St Agnes model village. And I understand you kids have your own ideas. Oh – and we can also use the special heated pool at the Spastics Society holiday place in Lanlivery, if I ring in the morning and fix a time. That'll come in handy in wet weather, especially as I'm afraid ordinary pools and the sea are far too cold for these children.'

Then we told him some of our ideas. A nature ramble. I suggested a sing-song, without thinking, then wished I hadn't because Burt and Anna could hardly speak, let alone sing, but to my astonishment they thought it was a great idea. Jane suggested riding, but Mr Kersey wasn't too sure they'd be able to manage that. Dave thought we could all go fishing even if it was only from the jetty, and had borrowed some rods. Mrs Kersey said we might like to go to the cinema in the second week, because *Fantasia* was back, showing with *The Sword in the Stone*.

That evening we were packed off early, because the kids had travelled a long way and were half asleep. We all agreed to turn up at Mr Kersey's at 9.30 a.m. the next day because of carrying wheelchairs onto and off the ferry and pushing them through towns. Actually Jane, who's a St John's Ambulance cadet and wants to be a missionary nurse like her aunt, promised to go at 7.30 a.m. to help get the kids washed and dressed but none of the rest of us could manage that, though both Podge and I get up early. She helps with milking, I do a paper round to the camp site and village.

We walked home together, cheerful but thoughtful. John's a real daredevil, he fears nobody and nothing, which I suppose is very useful if you want to take a TV camera to wars and danger areas. But now he said softly:

'Those kids have got real guts. I don't think I could stick being like them.'

'It seems so unfair,' I argued, 'that anyone should have so much going against them. I wonder *why?*'

'I don't suppose there's any easy answer,' Andy replied. I wondered if his dad, the vicar, would have been so honest. Jane just looked up shyly.

'I'm glad they like us and we can help them,' she murmured.

Podge nodded. 'We must give them the most super

time they've ever had,' she agreed. 'Beats me how Dave can understand Anna and Burt, though.'

'I think I'm beginning to,' Andy said. 'It's just the way you listen, and a bit of guesswork.'

Podge thought Andy and John might like to see their dog's new pups. I'd seen them, so I went on with Jane and got invited in by her aunt, who for some reason really approves of me. I suppose I *can* be ladylike, if I'm in the mood, and helping in Dad's shop as I do sometimes has taught me to be polite to people.

Miss Franklin quizzed us about the children. She seemed really interested. I told her all I could, cutting out the messier details of the tea party.

'I remember when I was a trainee nurse,' Miss Franklin said, 'there was a child in my ward who would be termed a cabbage. And a monster, too. He had a useless limp body, drooling dumb lips, dull eyes and a head far too large. He was more or less hidden away and the other nurses gave him the minimum possible attention. I wasn't so sure in my beliefs then, but I felt somehow God wanted me to love that child. To find time to cuddle him, sing to him, talk to him. Tell him about things, wheel him through the grounds. To treat him as an equal, valued by God. In those days we were much less enlightened about disability and I felt very embarrassed, but the feeling was so strong I just had to obey. And I was rewarded a thousand times. That boy began to come alive, to look at me, to smile. Even to try to speak.'

'Was he cured?' Jane asked hopefully. Miss Franklin shook her head.

'He died of kidney failure just before I left that ward,' she admitted. 'But at least he'd had two months of beginning to live. That's why I'm so thrilled now to see you children responding to these handicapped children with friendship instead of horror.'

She smiled at us, a string-bean of a woman in her early sixties, I suppose, her eyes were gentle and kind.

'Never ask why,' she continued. 'Waiting for answers, you may do nothing. Instead, ask what you can *do*.'

We both assured her that we would, and meant it, too.

'And tell Mr Kersey that I'd be very glad to help with bathing the children and getting them ready for bed in the evenings.'

Again we promised, and I was about to go when Miss Franklin offered me three books. I love reading, and I'll read almost anything, so I thanked her before I'd even looked at them. She smiled, amused.

'You should find them interesting, and maybe inspiring,' she promised.

I read one before bed (I read very fast). It was called *Hilary*, about a woman whose only movement was in a flicker of her big toe. She couldn't see or speak. With her big toe she operated the switch of a machine called a Possum which can be made to control all sorts of things, and typed letters and poems by electronic signals to a typewriter. It was fascinating, and if I hadn't been falling asleep very quickly by 9.30 p.m. I'd have started on the other books.

Monday was a gorgeous, sunny day and we were all up at the Kerseys' in plenty of time. Having a job to do helped a lot because it was a perfect sailing day and normally Podge and I would have spent a lot of it mooching about near the sailing club on the chance someone wanted a crew, which seldom happened in the week. Now, instead, we piled into the minibus, which had a hydraulic lift for the chairs, and went into Truro.

It's funny how a town you know well always seems nicer when you show it to visitors. We took the kids to the Cathedral, the Museum (where they used the goods lift) and some of our favourite shops before going down to catch the ferry. Some people stared at them, while others looked quickly away, but most of the shopkeepers were super. Somehow we paired off naturally with the kids – Dave and Andy with Burt, John and Jane with Anna, Podge and me with Stella. I admit I found Stella easiest to be friends with because she could talk and she was very bright. I thought if I couldn't use my arms or my legs, and my parents had dumped me, I'd hate everyone and everything and be really bitter, but Stella wasn't. Perhaps she'd been too young when it all happened to really notice and she'd got used to being handicapped. I don't know – and it wasn't the sort of thing you could ask – but anyway, she really seemed to enjoy every minute of life. If she was pretending, she pretended jolly well!

Mr Kersey had spoken to the ferry people in advance, and they'd got a bit of deck reserved for us. The crew and some strong holiday makers helped us down the steps with the chairs. I loved the ferries. It's a really pretty run, chugging up from Truro to Falmouth. The kids all came from a long-stay ward in a hospital in London so they'd had trips up and down the Thames a few times, but the Fal was really different for them. Of course, Andy kept on pointing out birds – a heronry, cormorants on the mooring buoys, moorhens and coots, the different kinds of gulls. Podge and I identified the dinghies we saw, and explained how the buoys marked a deep water channel.

'I wish I lived by the seaside,' Stella said wistfully, and I wondered where she *would* live when she was too old for the children's ward. Another ward for grown-ups, I supposed, or a Home if she was lucky. I had thought all disabled children went into Homes rather than wards, to be honest – that she was still in hospital when she wasn't strictly speaking *ill* took me by surprise and made me a bit angry, too. It didn't seem fair, or much fun.

'Daffy and I want to live here always,' Podge said. 'I'll run a sailing school and Daffy will help me in between writing best-selling novels. We'll both tour the world in our holidays, of course, but our home will be here. Even when Daffy marries Andy and I marry a tall, handsome millionaire with a yacht, we'll have a holiday home here and invite all our friends.'

She winked as she said it. Podge is always kidding, especially about Andy. Just because I like him – well, he's interesting – she keeps saying he'll grow up into a vicar like his Dad and I'll be the vicar's wife doing Good Deeds in the Parish. Sometimes when she teases me, I throw things at her. Usually, I just tease her right back, about Alan Carstairs. He's one of the stars of her swimming club, who lives near our village, and I think she secretly fancies him. Not that I'd call Podge the romantic type, but I caught her once writing her name and Alan's in her exercise book, and crossing out the matching letters, then counting the rest reciting, 'Love, Like, Hate, Adore.' So usually when she teases me about Andy, I kid her about Alan, the Future Olympic Hero. But I didn't this time, because I think Stella took us half-seriously.

'I could join you,' she said dreamily, 'when I finish art school. I'm going to be an artist – I can paint holding the brush in my mouth.'

We stared at her.

'Gosh,' Podge gasped, 'you'll have to show us. I can't draw for toffee – except boats.'

'I can only draw flowers, some animals, and ballet dancers,' I admitted.

Then we passed the King Harry Ferry which crosses the River Fal and John explained how it worked, with the chains and everything. Anna didn't say much, but her eyes were alive with interest all the time. Burt made lots of sounds and Dave translated, though I noticed Andy was getting the hang of understanding too. The Kerseys just produced food for all of us and left us to it.

There are too many hills in Falmouth. We hadn't the energy to push chairs to the castle or the beaches so we just went round the shops and the waterfront. The kids were fascinated by a T-shirt shop down one alley with hundreds of different slogans, and they all bought T-shirts. We also found out the hard way just how many shops had steps and the cafes were so crowded that finally we found one with a sort of tea-garden outside and had our afternoon drinks there.

Afterwards, we still had half an hour to spare before the ferry came, and the boys fancied fishing from the pier, or just watching the fishermen. I always think that's a dead loss – when I watch, every fish for miles immediately goes into hiding and nobody catches anything! So when Stella said she'd like to look in a few boutiques, I agreed to go with her. Anna was a bit drowsy, so we thought she'd better stay with the Kerseys and the boys, but Podge said she'd come along too, which surprised me because I'd always thought dressing up bored her. Funny how you sometimes don't really know even your best friends!

The first boutique we went to was the kind I hate, all wild punky disco gear and loud music, half dark and everyone in one big changing room. But the access was good and a girl with a bright purple stripe down the middle of her silver hair (honest!) was really nice to

Stella. Apparently the kids were allowed to choose their own clothes, I'm not sure where the money comes from but some sort of Government pay-out, I suppose. Stella normally had to order through a catalogue, and now she wanted to get something really special, for parties.

'But I can only spend up to £10,' she warned. As I get most of my gear second-hand from the Oxfam charity shop it seemed an impossibly high amount to me, but hardly anything in that place cost under £30. Beats me how these shops survive when so many teenagers are unemployed!

Anyway the girl went out back and returned with her arms full of 'Seconds'.

'Put aside for the end-of-season sale,' she explained, 'but take your pick now. Nothing over £10.'

Eagerly Stella watched as the girl, Podge and I, held up garments. Some were just far too big, and some so way-out that we got the giggles.

'Hey, I like this,' I said suddenly, holding up a filmy, floaty golden thing that made me think of some romantic 1920s heroine.

'It's very feminine, and it'd fall nicely sitting down. And it's only £6,' the salesgirl agreed. Stella wasn't so sure.

'I'd really like to wear a slinky catsuit,' she said, 'but I don't think I curve enough in the right places yet.'

'I curve too much in the wrong places!' Podge giggled. 'How about this?'

'This' was hideous! Even the salesgirl had to laugh. I mean, who wants to look like a futuristic robot?

'Here's another possible. This is really super.'

I'd pounced again. The bodice was all glittering stretchy material, fitting like a leotard. In fact it was a leotard, except there was also a diaphanous, floaty divided skirt. The colours are hard to describe, sort of

sea colours mingled, not quite blue, not quite tur-
quoise.

'Eight pounds,' the salesgirl said. 'Actually, this is
special, it was made for a customer's kid who was going
to be in a dancing show, then she broke her ankle. It's
really a good buy.'

'It's gorgeous!' Stella breathed. 'I'd like to try it on,
but dressing me is such a drag.'

'Take it home and bring it back if it doesn't fit,' the
girl suggested. So we decided to.

We still had ten minutes, even counting time to get
back to the pier.

'Let's go into Gear Change,' Podge suggested. 'I'm
after a dance dress.'

Gear Change sells good, second-hand stuff and it was
only just up the road from the boutique, so we went in.

'What dance?' I asked, and Podge actually blushed.

'The Carnival one. From the hints Alan was
throwing out yesterday I think he's going to ask me.'

'How romantic!' Stella breathed. 'What sort of a
dance is it? And who's Alan?'

I gave Podge a wide-eyed look, but she just said
casually, 'Oh, a friend from the Swimming Club.'

'The dance is really classy – full evening dress,' I
explained. 'There's a band and everything. But tickets
cost a packet.'

'Alan's Dad's on the committee,' Podge said. 'He's
expected to go. I think they get in free.'

There were lots of pretty long dresses in size 14, but
Podge didn't fancy any of them. So she decided she'd
make one instead, and we were just about to go off and
look for a pattern when we realized that if we didn't
dash, we'd miss the ferry. So we went belting down to
the quay, Podge pushing Stella's chair and me running
ahead through all the wandering holidaymakers

yelling 'Gangway, gangway — sorry, we've got to catch a ferry!'

A wheelchair in a crowd can be pretty lethal! We arrived in a panting rush, and the grinning ferry man loaded Stella, while the boys pretended to look superior.

'Can't trust you girls out on your own,' Andy said, keeping a straight face. 'Tut, tut!'

'Thought the tide would turn, we waited so long,' John agreed.

Even Burt managed to say, ever so clearly, 'Tut! Tut!'

All the way back to Truro, they kept teasing us about it, but we didn't care. We were too happy. I don't know why. It had been a perfectly ordinary sort of day, really, but somehow being with the kids had made it special. Just looking round the shops was a treat to them, so were silly things like actually living in an ordinary house and seeing food prepared in a kitchen instead of coming from a heated hospital trolley. Stella told me about the ward as we drove back in the minibus, and it sounded pretty depressing, even though there were posters on the walls and a bit of a balcony where they could sit out. She said most of the other children were severely mentally handicapped too, or seemed to be. Both Anna and Burt were thought to be retarded, but nobody was quite sure how much, because their physical and speech handicaps made assessment difficult.

'I go to a local Special School,' she explained, 'but they just go to the hospital one. It's not as hard — I mean, they don't have exams like we do. I type my lessons on an electric typewriter with a mouthstick.'

'School's fun,' she added, with a rueful little smile. 'I've got lots of friends there. But when they go home

I wish I was going with them. Not back to the ward, where the only people I can really talk to are the staff, and they haven't much time. And in the holidays I'm so bored! But, sorry, I shouldn't be grousing at you. It's not your fault, and I suppose I'm quite lucky really . . .'

I couldn't see how, but I let it go. And that evening, I really felt grateful for my own room in my own home, which I'd taken totally for granted before. It's not a spectacular room, and all the furniture's second-hand, but at least I can fill it with all my own clutter and go in there when I want to read or write, or even sulk! Mum moans about how untidy it is and makes me clean it every so often, but it's my private place and neither she nor Dad would come in without knocking or asking. The most privacy Stella ever got in the hospital was if they pulled the curtains round her bed, and she said some of them thought she was making a fuss when she asked for these to be pulled while they dressed her. They usually didn't bother, even though there were boys and girls in the same ward. I don't think I'm a prude, but I thought that was awful, not being able to have any sort of privacy. Not even in the most personal things! I mean – well, going to the loo. She knows when she needs to go, and in Falmouth Podge and I had taken her to a disabled one. We'd had to take her knickers down for her, lift her on and then I'd supported her there, but at least we'd shut the door. But she said, in the ward, a nurse would sometimes support her and talk to another nurse through the open doorway at the same time. Honestly! I'd always thought being disabled just meant you couldn't walk, or use your arms or your eyes or something – not that you had to face all sorts of horrid little humiliations as well. It made my blood boil!

Mum says I get too involved in other people's

problems sometimes, and she worries because I'm so busy trying to put the world to rights I forget unimportant things like homework. But I think she's pleased and proud of me, too, in a cockeyed sort of way, when I start my campaigning. She often backs me up, and calls me 'Little Mother of all the World'.

Up there in the quiet of my room that night, I decided I was going to Do Something to make life better for kids like Stella. I didn't know what or how, but I was going to jolly well find a way!

CHAPTER 3

ME AND MY
BIG MOUTH

On Tuesday, Podge and I were 'off duty', so was Jane, who was going to Plymouth with her aunt. The boys were going to the Model Village with the kids (I'd been before, so I didn't mind missing that).

Podge and I spent the best part of the day nailing together a frame, and lashing the fertilizer drums to it, three each side, like catamaran floats. Then we dragged it down to the creek where it comes up against her dad's land, and launched it. The raft floated OK, and climbing on, we started to paddle down the creek. Of course, when the rotten drums decided to become unlashed, they did it right up near the club where the Corsairs were having a water-fight (a bit like jousting, only with dinghies and water pistols). They stopped, and laughed themselves silly as Podge and I, abandoning what was left of the raft, started towing the drums ashore one by one.

'Win a race with that?' Luke jeered, and Carolyn got her own back on my by gloating, 'Now who can't tie knots?'

I pretended to laugh with them.

'Never mind,' I said heartily. 'Back to the drawing board!'

Teasing's never so satisfactory if the person you're trying to make fun of thinks it's funny too, so they quickly gave up on me and, led by Sarah, even helped get the rest of the drums and the framework in. The Corsairs can be quite nice if they're in the mood and I suppose they were prepared to be gracious because I'd already fallen flat on my face!

Podge suggested using one of her dad's huge tractor inner tubes as a raft base, but I thought he wasn't likely to let me borrow a blow-uppable one, because they're awfully dear.

'I'll try making something with ordinary inner tubes and polystyrene offcuts,' I said. 'I know where I can get lots of those free.'

But there wasn't time left to try anything that day, and in the evening, instead of working out a design, I read the second of Miss Franklin's books, called *Take my Hands,* all about a paraplegic lady doctor in India who did surgery on the hands of leprosy patients. I was beginning to see that for some people, disability wasn't an unbearable burden, it was a challenge, and it certainly wasn't the end to a happy and constructive life. I supposed that was why Jane's aunt had lent me the books, so I could think that way when I was with the kids. If so, she had the right idea – I stopped feeling sorry about the things they couldn't do, and started to try to think of things they could do. Especially Stella. She'd talked about painting, so I dug out all my old paints.

I don't know why, but whenever I get a sudden craze for painting, I seem to get boxes of cheap watercolour paints, use them a bit, get bored with it, and shove them in a cupboard somewhere. Then I forget them, so next time I want to paint, I go out and buy some more. By hunting all over the house, I managed to find four part-used boxes of watercolours, ten part-used pots of the ready-mixed kind of poster paint and six rather scruffy brushes. Plus some quite decent pencils with the handles only a bit chewed (when I'm writing or drawing and I get stuck, I chew the pen or pencil. Mum used to say I'd end up with lead poisoning). I hadn't any plain paper, but Mum let me cut up some lining paper left over from decorating the attic.

It would be a start for Stella, at any rate.

Next day, Wednesday, it poured. Andy and John were doing their turn helping at their Camera Club's summer exhibition, and Dave was helping Mr Trevanson, so it was just us girls with the kids.

'A swimming day,' Mr Kersey acknowledged, 'and then a stay in and do things day.'

There's a nice pool in Truro plus the Leisure Centres at Carn Brea and St Austell, but we went further afield, to Churchtown Farm. As it was all designed for disabled people, the pool had easy access and was a lot warmer than most – like a bath, after the creek!

We sang all the way there. Even Jane, who's got a sweet, soft voice, joined in, and the Kerseys. Stella could sing properly though not very loudly, and the others just made the best noises they could. I'm a bit of a bighead, I admit, and I like the sound of my own voice. I may be useless at gym and athletics but I sing solo in the choir and I'm always top in English and Team Leader of the Junior Debating Society. I knew in my heart that thought I felt sorry for Anna and Burt, and friendly towards Stella, it was in a superior sort of way. I wondered how it must feel to them, not to have anything they were best at. The thought made me feel churned up and guilty inside – the fact that I was half happy with them, half having to pretend because I really choose people more like me as friends. I even feel a bit superior to Podge sometimes, because she's fat. It's hard to want to be a nice person and always think kind thoughts, but you find you just can't.

In the water, though, I soon forgot my guilty self-analysis. I love swimming, and I enjoy teaching swimming. The kids all wore swimsuits with built-in buoyancy – we towed or supported them. Jane played in the shallow end with Anna, who was a bit frightened, while Podge and I took Burt and Stella. Mr Kersey only let them stay in for just under half an hour. I think he was worried they might get tired or cold, despite the warmth of the water. We were allowed to stay in a bit longer and show off, duck-diving, somersaulting and doing handstands. Then, with the rain still bucketing down, we drove off and had our picnic in the minibus, looking over the Fowey estuary, which was very pretty in a bedraggled sort of way.

Afterwards, we went to the Kerseys and sat in their big lounge. Anna, Burt, Podge and Jane watched television – according to Stella, they get square eyes in the ward, the television is on so much. But there was a good old film showing, a sea adventure, right up Podge's street, and as Jane doesn't have a telly at home she was glad to watch too.

Stella and I painted. Mr Kersey rigged a temporary easel on the tray which fits to her chair, and pinned paper to it. I'd found the paints and we put a little pot of water on the tray.

I rushed out into the garden to pick some wild flowers (it's that kind of garden, more pretty weeds than ordered plants in rows) and painted them. But I didn't do much, I was too busy watching Stella control the brush with her mouth. Anna's birthday was at the end of the month and the picture was to be a present for her, so Stella painted what she said Anna liked best.

Ponies. Ponies running down a beach, kicking up the spray. Now I absolutely hate trying to draw horses; their legs always seem to go wrong, but hers were all in proportion and they moved right. They were so alive they almost came running off the paper and that's quite something for any thirteen-year-old artist. Most of the kids I know who can use their hands couldn't paint such real ponies.

'I learn by looking at pictures in books,' Stella explained, 'but one day, I'm determined to go to a proper art school.'

Her eyes had a far-away, wistful look as if she already realized her chances of doing things were slim, and she'd need superhuman determination to get where she wanted to be.

I told her how I wanted to be a writer; how I'd won a couple of children's competition prizes and had letters and jokes published in comics. But it was easier for me; writers can get ordinary jobs and write in their spare time, they don't have to be trained.

'I don't expect I'll get a novel published until I'm quite old and Know About Life,' I admitted, grinning. 'So I'll do a secretarial course. That way I can earn my living and type my own stories.'

'Tell us a story one day,' Stella urged. Not that I needed any urging! I promised I would.

I didn't start that evening though, because I'd promised to meet Andy. He'd dashed in on his way to catch the bus in the morning and said he'd got some exciting news. I'd been wondering what it was all day!

It could be to do with sailing – perhaps the doctor had said he was well enough to start again, and he was getting a boat? Or maybe he was going somewhere and wanted me to come too. Or it could be about singing – we both belong to our school's Cornish Heritage Club which tries to preserve the Cornish language, folk songs and dances, and we both sing in Cornish. Sometimes we do things at folk festivals.

My mind was full of all sorts of exciting might-be's when I went to meet him from the bus. He was on his own, because John had stayed to see a film. Perhaps I was too het up and excited.

Because what happened that evening makes me feel so crawly with shame, I don't honestly want to write it down. It makes me seem so mean, petty, nasty and stupid and I don't really think I'm like that – well, not usually. But it's important, so I'll write it down quickly and get it over with and if you've ever said and done something stupid to upset *your* best friend, perhaps you'll understand and not hate me too much!

You see, when Andy's news turned out to be that the Junior Church were going to do a beach barbecue for the kids, I felt really huffy.

I said, 'Great, they'll love it!' because I knew they would. But something inside me stiffened angrily. *We* were the kids' special friends, *we* could think up enough for them to do. The Junior Church were just sticking their oar in to show what good little Christians they were. Instead of being pleased, I just felt cross and I suppose a bit jealous, because I hadn't thought of the idea first.

Andy didn't notice that I'd gone quiet – always a danger sign with me. He was too pleased and excited.

'It was my idea,' he said happily. 'I felt the other kids would like to be involved. They jumped at it! We're going to do sausages and beefburgers, with hot soup or coke, down on Lowen Beach. It's tomorrow, starting 6 p.m.. You'll come, won't you?'

'No thanks,' I replied coldly. 'Junior Church just isn't my scene.'

The smile died from his face and his eyes had a wounded look. I felt a bit guilty, knowing how it hurts when someone treads on my ideas. Trying to make amends, I just made things worse.

'Look,' I said. 'It's different for you, being the Vicar's son. You've *got* to like that sort of thing.'

'I go to Junior Church because I happen to like being a Christian, I like the other kids, and I enjoy it,' Andy answered, and now *he* was stiff and cold. 'Not because of what my dad is. And I get pretty fed up with the way you keep digging at Junior Church and treating it like one big joke.'

That was unfair. I avoided Junior Church, but I hardly ever knocked it. So I got angry.

'I don't dig at it, but I jolly well could!' I snapped back. 'Half the kids are drips and the rest are hypocrites.'

As soon as I said it, I wished I could un-say it. It was just anger talking, not what I really thought. But Andy jumped down my throat.

'I don't know if I'm supposed to be a drip or a hypocrite,' he snarled, 'but I'm sure you wouldn't want to be friends with either. Forget the barbecue – we'll survive without you!'

Then he turned and walked away, fast. For a minute, I just stood there. It had all blown up so quickly, I felt bewildered and shattered. In just a few horrid words, and for no good reason at all, I'd made the nicest boy I knew into my enemy. I couldn't understand why I'd been so nasty, and I hated myself. My temper always has flared up very quickly, but it dies just as fast and I end up feeling stricken and grovellingly apologetic. It was like that now. I tried to make myself blame Andy – it would have hurt less if I could sulk and resent him. But I couldn't.

'Andy!' I yelled, running after him. 'Oh, Andy, please, I'm sorry, I didn't mean what I said!'

He didn't turn.

'Why say it, then?' he asked, walking on without looking at me.

'I don't know!' I wailed. 'I was jealous, cross and stupid, and I didn't stop to think! Please, Andy . . .'

He stopped then, and turned. I was crying and I always go red and spotty when I cry, but I didn't care.

'It's all right, Daffy,' Andy muttered, trying to smile. 'Forget it.'

But it wasn't all right; there was still pain deep in his eyes. I wanted to see him really smile at me again, and I knew only one way to try. Daffy by name, daft by nature . . .

I don't think he expected me to fall on my knees in the mud at his feet (and there was *worse* than mud in that lane, the cows use it to cross to Mr Pengilly's milking parlour!).

'I cringe, I grovel,' I howled. 'I am trying to be most abjectly humble and truly sorry and if only you'll believe I didn't mean it, Andy, I will even come to Junior Church next Sunday!'

'Oh, Daffy, you are a twit!' Andy said, but he reached down to drag me to my feet and the smile on his face was much more real. There was even some of the old warmth back in his eyes.

'Your Mum'll have a fit if you go home like that,' he said, and I realized that apart from my muddy legs, I'd managed to splash quite a bit of mud and probably cow dung onto my skirt as well. I shrugged and said I'd dive into the creek and wash it off that way, but he shook his head.

'Come home with me. Mum'll run you a bath and lend you another skirt while you wash yours out and leave it on our line overnight,' he insisted. 'And I'll make you a milk shake or something.'

'I can have a bath at home . . .' I began, but Andy said softly,

'I'm trying to grovel too, I just don't do it as spectacularly as you. I want to make amends for being so uptight. It's just that when you really believe in something . . .'

'And someone kicks it, it hurts,' I finished for him. 'Andy, I honestly wasn't knocking *Jesus*, and I'm really, truly sorry about what I said to you, it's just that . . .'

I shut up then, scared I'd put my foot in it again.

'It's just some Christians you can't stand!' Andy exclaimed, but he was grinning now.

We agreed to let his Mum think I'd just fallen over – anything else would be too complicated. She's the mother hen type anyway. She took one look at me, said, 'You poor child!' and went to run me a bath and find an old wrap-round skirt of hers I could borrow. When I said I'd take my skirt home and wash it there, she wouldn't hear of it, but insisted it could go in the washing-machine with her stuff, and I could pick it up, dried and ironed, tomorrow. It seemed a lot of bother for her, and I felt rather guilty, but at least I could bring her some flowers to say thanks, when I picked up the skirt.

And I must admit I was glad to wash off all the muck. I'd looked a real mess, and I hadn't exactly smelt sweet either. I suppose a sensible, dignified girl wouldn't have done such a crazy thing, but then I'm *me* and anyway, it had worked! I still shivered, though, to think that in a couple of stupid, angry minutes I could have lost Andy's friendship maybe for ever.

When I emerged all sweet-smelling from the

bathroom, his Mum explained she'd got to go to a ladies' meeting and her husband was in his study working on a sermon, so Andy could entertain me and walk me home. It was still only about a quarter to eight.

When she'd gone, Andy and I just sat tongue-tied for a bit. Then he said awkwardly, 'Daf, I won't hold you to what you said about coming to Junior Church. I shouldn't have tried to shove it down your throat. I didn't mean to preach . . .'

'And I didn't mean to be so beastly. I was only getting at people like Carolyn, really,' I admitted. 'She is a bit much. But I said I'll come and I will, if you'll have me. Though I bet everyone will either look at me sideways and think I've come to make fun of them, or they'll laugh themselves silly.'

'They'd better not!' Andy growled. Then he looked embarrassed. 'But there's no point in you coming just to please me,' he added.

'It really isn't just that,' I said slowly. 'I think I do want to believe. But Jesus expects a sort of total takeover, doesn't he? And I'm not really willing to give up every bit of me.'

I hesitated a bit, then, trying to get my thoughts straightened out. 'But I would like to be nicer than I am,' I continued after a minute. 'I'd like to . . .' What I wanted to say sounded so pious I shuddered, but went on defiantly, 'I'd like to please God.'

Andy didn't laugh, or even look surprised. He just said softly, 'Oh, Fran, you are nice. You're the nicest girl I know. I only wish I could think of the right things to say to you about Jesus'.

I rather liked him calling me Fran. I've been Daffy so long I'd almost forgotten I'd got a real name. Fran is short for Franchys, which means 'Freedom' in Cornish, and Dad's always said it was a well-chosen name for me, because if ever a kid was determined to be free, I'm it! But I also liked Andy's honesty. He could have waffled on piously for hours.

So I grinned.

'Let Junior Church have a go at convincing me,' I suggested, 'and we can walk home the long way, through Badger's Copse, see if we can spot The Hulk.'

'Great!'

The Hulk is a big boar badger. All the farm dogs are scared rigid of him. At one time Mr James, the farmer who then owned Dallys Farm, wanted to gas the sett because he said the badgers gave the cows TB. There was a big argy-bargy about it, with Andy and me joining the vigil of naturalists who were fighting it. In the end it turned out that Mr James had been grazing his cattle on somebody else's land, and so he decided it would be tactful to forget about the badgers. But that's another story!

Anyway, Andy got his camera and told his Dad, then we went. It was exciting in the copse at twilight, noises and sudden little movements everywhere. But no Hulk. We didn't wait near the sett, because I had promised to be home by nine, and as we came back onto the road a big sports car flashed past us.

'Idiot!' I shrieked, because he was going far too fast. Then I saw it was Carolyn's mum in the passenger seat, but it wasn't her Dad driving. He was in France until Saturday; Carolyn had boasted as usual about his Important Business Trip.

'There goes one big reason for putting up with Carolyn and Peter,' Andy said cryptically, and added, 'They're staying with their cousins tonight.'

'Oh,' was all I could manage. The year before, we'd had my unspeakable second cousins, Cuthbert and

Jewell, with us for a whole month. Compared to them, even Carolyn was angelic. But when I'd blown my top, Mum had explained they were with us while their parents both made a last ditch attempt to salvage their marriage. And they were awful because they were worried sick.

'Poor things,' I muttered. Andy nodded. We walked the last bit in silence, then at my gate Andy asked.

'You will come to the barbecue?'

This time, only too grateful for a second chance, I didn't hesitate. 'Yes, please!'

'I'll call for you,' Andy promised, then he waved and was gone.

I went in. Dad and Mum were arguing in a peaceable sort of way about something obscure and political. We have lots of arguments in our house, but not many rows. I tried to picture Mum going out with another man, or Dad taking every possible opportunity to go gallivanting off, and couldn't. Relieved, I told them a bit about my day and explained my change of skirt. I also confessed I was going to the Junior Church barbecue and even Junior Church.

'Only just to give it a trial, though,' I added firmly.

Mum and Dad exchanged pleased little looks. They've been trying to get me involved with church for years. But I went up to my room before they could start asking questions. I might be able to share some of my thoughts with Andy, but I wasn't quite ready to share them with Mum and Dad.

Before going to bed, to sort of unwind myself, I read the end of the last book Miss Franklin had lent me. This one was called *Still Life* about a dancer who was paralysed by polio and though she had to spend her nights in an iron lung, became a mouth-painter and sold her stuff internationally. I decided to ask Miss

Franklin if I could lend it to Stella, to encourage her. And I did pray, that night!

CHAPTER 4

BEACHCOMBING

Thursday is Dad's half-holiday. It's also everyone-do-jobs-around-the-house day. I have set jobs I must do anyway, like cleaning my room, washing up, helping with the cooking and doing the vegetables. Then there's 'optionals' I often do because I like them, and not for pay — like decorating, and demolishing things, and building walls and helping Dad put roofing felt on the shed. Then there's extra-pocket-money jobs like polishing lino and furniture, as I'd done on Sunday, washing the car, cleaning the windows, cutting the grass.

This Thursday, because it was raining again, I did some wallpaper scraping in the back room. Sometimes that's an easy job because the wallpaper peels off in big strips if the room is damp. But this room is so dry, and nobody had ever taken paper off, they'd just put more on top, and painted on it. I'd get some off and find another layer, and with the paint, the paper wouldn't soak through properly. Still, I didn't mind because I had my tranny tuned to Radio 2 and danced as I scraped. I also stopped whenever I liked for coffee or coke. Then at about 3 p.m. I clocked off and curled up in my room with an exercise book, to write a story. I got a bit carried away and knew it would have to be a serial.

It was all about the Tests a Princess had to take on an alien planet. As it was for the kids, I'd made the Princess handicapped. She had a twin brother who was healthy and normal but rather a twit and a ditherer so she had to be the brains and courage while he provided legs and strength. Little by little some of her sense and fearlessness rubbed off on him, while she, by having to try to do things nobody had ever asked her to do before, gained strength. I decided that it would be in five episodes, each with a cliff-hanger ending, so I could give the kids one each day.

It was rather nice to have some quiet time all to myself. I was still a bit shaken by how nasty I'd been to Andy, how I'd nearly lost his friendship. There'd been other times when I've frightened myself like that, times when I'd been really horrid to Mum and Dad, screaming at them, sulking – even breaking a plate once by throwing it in sheer temper. It's as though someone who's not really me takes over, and afterwards I hate myself.

I told myself in future I'd count to ten before I said anything, ever, but deep inside I knew it wouldn't work. I think I even knew what *would* work, but I refused to admit it even to myself. You see, I didn't mind being on the same side as Jesus – he had a lot of very good ideas, and was a brave, good man. But I didn't want him interfering in my life.

One of my favourite poems was the one that says:
   'I am the master of my fate,
   I am the captain of my soul.'
That's how I wanted to be. Strong, proud, independent. Free! I told myself I could manage my own life, and I was still trying to totally convince myself when, just after 5.30, Andy came round. By then the rain had stopped, and he said his Dad and Mum were taking

some of the barbecue stuff down to Lowen Beach in their car, and would give us a lift. He was cheerful, as if our argument had never happened, or was forgiven and forgotten. Thank goodness!

'We've managed to fix a boat trip for the kids, in that big old boat of Mr Curnow's,' he explained. 'They'll actually sail!'

'Great!'

This time, I was determined to share his enthusiasm all the way. And I did think it was great. Sailing's a thousand times more exciting than a ferry to Falmouth and the kids would be quite safe in the big lugger, providing nobody dropped them while getting on board!

We were the first to arrive, but Mrs Curnow, who runs the café while her husband runs a sailing school, had already set up the barbecue for us. We were getting all the drinks from her and any extras. I say 'we' but of course I was really only a guest – or thought I was.

Andy's mum had the sausages, beefburgers, oil, onions and soup. The rolls came a few minutes later, with Sarah and her Mum. Sarah teased me about my raft-making, but in quite a friendly way. I could see she was nervous.

'What are the kids like?' she asked me. 'I would have helped before, but I was scared I wouldn't know what to say or do, or that I'd be shocked and they'd know it . . . Can they do anything? Can we talk to them?'

'You won't get a brilliant conversation – in fact, hardly any conversation at all that you can understand – out of Burt or Anna,' I admitted, 'but Stella's just like you and me, apart from her physical handicap. We'll have to help feed them, by the way, but it's a laugh, really.'

She looked a bit reassured.

To save time, we started splitting rolls. Podge, Jenny (Luke's big sister), Jane, Luke and the kids arrived, and two boys and a girl I knew by sight but not well – Sam, Isaac and Rachel Polgooth. They brought guitars. The Curnow kids also came over to help, bringing stuff from their Mum's cafe.

Even though it was evening, there were quite a lot of people on the beach swimming, going out to or coming back from boats, windsurfing. I could see a waterskier far over the other side of Carrick Roads, a faint speck towards St Just.

Mr Curnow had suggested we do the boat trip first. It was just as well, because the wind was dying. Another boy and girl turned up in time to take the kids onto the jetty where the lugger was moored. The adults went out to load them, which was going to be the tricky bit. The idea was to have half an hour's sail, then come back for the barbecue. The boat could only comfortably take about nine, so Andy and I volunteered to stay behind. Andy was looking a bit worried.

'Mum, did you invite the other disabled kids from Red Cross House too?' he asked, and his mother nodded.

'Yes,' she explained, 'but they won't be coming until about seven, because they've been to Penzance for the day. It'll be just the disabled children, the Red Cross junior helpers aren't free this evening.'

'Then there really ought to be more of us to help,' Andy muttered.

'It was short notice, and the time before the Carnival's difficult for a lot of people,' his mother said cheerfully. 'So much to do, make, practise. Stop worrying and turn some sausages or they'll be burned on the outside and uncooked in the middle. There's at least one of you to each child, not counting grown-ups.'

'We'll manage fine,' I promised, turning onions until my eyes streamed. Andy gave me a little, shamefaced grin.

'I want everything to go perfectly,' he admitted. 'I wanted to impress you with how super Junior Church kids are. So half of them don't turn up!'

'Oh, they'll be in Guides and Scouts and lumbered with other things,' I reassured him. 'Not their fault.'

I was part right, too. Dave came whizzing down on his bike, with Tim and Mike Spargo, just before the Red Cross kids arrived. They were still in paint-stained gear from working on a float, but set to happily, unloading the children. We were serving the first grub as the others landed.

It was a super evening (and to think I'd so nearly missed out on it!) We had our grub, then the Polgooths played their guitars and we sang as we sat in the warm evening air watching the late boats drifting slowly home on a sea getting more like a mirror every moment. They sang a few folk gospel songs that everyone knew, and then they had a go at any song the kids requested. And they were really good. I was surprised and a bit jealous to see Sarah and Stella chatting like they were old friends – but this time, I was determined to shove any nasty feelings aside before they could do any harm! After a while I even managed to feel honestly glad that Stella had a new friend, and really delighted when Mike Spargo also chatted to her.

'You know, Andy,' I mused as we sat together eating the last few sausages, 'it seems awful the kids should go back from this to that miserable hospital. I wish we could set up a proper homely home down here in Cornwall. Or even give more holidays to them and kids like them. There must be hundreds stuck in hospitals.'

'I was talking to Dad,' Andy whispered, 'and we got

this idea of a scheme where a local Junior Church links up with kids in a hospital near them. He's contacting one near our kids' hospital. Then they keep regular contact, and raise money to send a mixed group on holiday here. We raise money to help put them up somewhere, and act as hosts. Don't let on, though, in case it doesn't come off.'

'There's only one thing wrong with that idea,' I whispered back. 'It's so brilliant I should have thought of it!'

Andy laughed. Then another thought struck me.

'Would I be able to help? I don't go to Junior Church,' I said. 'It won't be just for Christian helpers?' I added in a very small voice.

'Of course you could help,'' said Andy seriously, 'But being a Christian is great, honest! What have you got against it?'

What? I wasn't sure. I could have said I wanted to be free to make my own decisions, not to have to do this or that because it was in the Bible. But deep down I knew that was a lousy excuse. Andy wasn't a sort of biblically-programmed robot, after all! In fact the more I thought about it, the more my easy reasons turned into excuses. So I hurriedly turned the subject back to the disabled kids.

'We'll have to think up fund-raising ideas,' I said quickly. 'Is there anything that hasn't been sponsored yet?'

'Bubble gum blowing?' Andy suggested. Then, realizing what I was up to, he grinned and added, 'But I won't forget my question!'

I smiled sweetly.

'Winkle picking,' I replied, then hissed, 'Too bad. You won't get an answer until I can think up a good one!'

But Andy was on form. Quick as a shot he argued back.

'There isn't a good answer to not being a Christian. I'm not trying to convert you, Fran, honest – it's just ... well, when you know you're into something good you want to share it with your friends ...'

'Thanks,' I said, because I knew he meant it.

'Look, if I really want to get to know Jesus properly, with all my heart ... I'll tell you first. If I have questions, I promise I'll ask you. But I won't be conned into anything!'

'OK,' he said, and smiled and squeezed my hand. 'So, back to a safe subject. What about backwards roller skating?'

'Conkers? Stone-skimming? Hiccups?' I suggested, warming to my subject, and when Mike Spargo shouted 'Rain!' I said, 'Sponsored rain? Smashing idea, we'd make a fortune in Cornwall!'

'The girl's nuts!' Mike said, staring at me, and all the others laughed.

'He means it's starting to rain, idiot!' Podge explained patiently, and she was right. So we grabbed everything – kids first, then barbecue stuff, and packed up. It was 8.15 p.m. anyway.

By the time we were ready to go, it was chucking it down. Often, when the wind drops and the tide changes, the rain comes in. Mr Mackay said they'd drop me off at home.

It occurred to me as we drove back that I ought to play fair. I'd more or less promised to really think about Christianity after all, and I shouldn't make an uninformed decision. As the biggest noise in the Junior Debating Society for two years, I'd learnt to look at things from every side and do some research.

But I hadn't read a Bible for years, hadn't even

heard it read, except the bits we had to put up with at school in Assembly and Religious Education. (And I usually whispered to my friends during assembly and did my homework secretly in RE because we didn't have a proper teacher, it was a once-a-week 'filler' lesson and the teacher stuck with it couldn't really care less what we did.)

I decided perhaps I should borrow Mum's Bible. Not that I was really keen. What I did remember about the Bible was boring, old-fashioned, peculiar English! But it seemed only fair I should find out more about Jesus and the Bible was the obvious place to look.

Unfortunately, Mum reads her Bible often – I knew I'd not be able to just sneak it up to my room, I'd have to ask to borrow it. So I did, and she smiled, obviously delighted.

'I've got a Good News one that's been waiting two years for you,' she said, going to her Present Cupboard (we all have one totally confidential cupboard or drawer that nobody else would dream of touching). 'Here.'

It was a huge paperback, with colour illustrations. I felt a bit of a cheat, taking it.

'I'm still not a Christian,' I protested. 'I'm just looking into it.'

'Fine,' Dad said. 'People who approach a subject with an open mind and make a free, rational decision with all their brain and heart in it, usually stick to it. Go on, read all about it! It's more interesting than you think. But pray, too.'

Actually, I often do pray, anyway. Especially for people I love, and for peace, and for sick people. But I knew what Dad meant – pray to understand the reality behind this great tome in my hands. At least, I could tell from a quick glance that it was readable. And if all else failed, it would come in handy for pressing flowers!

As I went upstairs, I heard Dad say, 'That young Andy must be a good influence,' and I giggled at Mum's reply.

'Shush!' she said fiercely. 'Do you want to put her off him?'

But she needn't have worried!

When I woke on Friday morning, it had stopped raining and there was that misty haze that promises a really scorching day. With only eight days to go to the Regatta, I would have liked to get on with making my raft. Dad had brought me some scrap polystyrene from a Truro electrical goods firm (they use it for packing), and the inner tubes chucked out by the tyre people. But I was on the rota for helping, along with Andy and Jane. The Kerseys decided we'd take advantage of the good weather and go over to Perranporth beach.

On the way, we stopped at the riding school. Not to ride, but so that Anna could see the horses. It had got to be a standing joke – every horse we passed when we were out in the minibus, she'd make excited noises, clearly wanting to stop and be introduced! So this time we took a bag of rather worse for wear apples, cut into small pieces. These we tipped into Anna's lap, and the more even-tempered ponies were brought over to feed. You should have seen Anna's face when a great, gentle pony head bent to nibble a few pieces of apple! She was thrilled to bits, and we stayed for about half an hour, just making friends with the horses. Then we drove on, parked as close as we could to Perranporth beach and manoeuvred the chairs down on to the sand.

Perranporth is my favourite beach. It's long and sandy, with super dunes and caves. In winter, sand-yachts race there, and sometimes people hang-glide.

You can also see the gliders going up from their airfield on the cliffs between St Agnes and Perranporth. There's warm shallow beach pools, and exciting surf — though you really do have to obey the red flags, because sometimes there's a dangerous rip-tide and the lifesavers are forever having to go in after idiots who ignore the signs and get into trouble.

But for the kids, the sand was the really important thing. They couldn't go in the water because it was too cold, so we made sandcastles, aeroplanes and rocket ships. I say we, but of course I mean Andy, Jane and me. The best we could offer the kids as participants, not just watchers, was to lift them out of their chairs and let them wriggle on the sand or be buried in it, which Mrs Kersey wasn't keen on for fear of sand up eyes and noses. Stella and Burt could do some wriggling, but Anna couldn't — she had to be lifted in her chair often during the day for fear of pressure sores, and I understood the Kerseys had also got a night nurse for the fortnight, just to keep a watch on the kids and turn them in bed if needed.

We couldn't get the wheelchairs to the rock pools where the really interesting creatures were, so we decided to make our own pool on the beach. We dug a hole, lined it with the bit of plastic we'd been using as a picnic cloth, put lots of stones round the edge to weigh the plastic down, and more pebbles, stones and sand on the bottom. Then we filled it with water, and collected weed and shells to pretty it up. Then with nets and jam jars, we went foraging. Some things, like limpets and sea anemones, we couldn't prize off the rocks. We didn't want to force them too hard in case we hurt them, so we concentrated on easier prey — little fish, crabs, a hermit crab with his shell attached, and shrimps. Andy said from a naturalist's point of view it was a highly unrepresentative rock pool but the kids loved it.

Burt had been interested by all the birds when we went on the ferry to Falmouth, but he was really turned on by the pool. Even without Dave to translate his enthusiastic noises, you could see it in his eyes. Andy knelt beside him, fishing up things for closer inspection, and explaining them like he was a professor sharing his pet subject with a bright and eager student.

I thought of that long, dull hospital ward which I'd never seen, but Stella had described in all its yukkiness. Surely they could find a little space for an aquarium? Not boring old goldfish that just swim round gulping at you through the glass, but tadpoles that turn into frogs; newts, and ugly vicious nymphs that crawl up sticks and miraculously become beautiful dragonflies. In the meantime, he could have his own sea aquarium!

Caught by one of my brilliant ideas, I told the others I wouldn't be a moment, and raced up the beach. Aquariums cost money but catering size packs of ice cream and margarine come in big containers which often get thrown away. Mum had scrounged some from the Peveran Arms which we used as lunch boxes. A few even came in transparent plastic.

I looked in the beach café, but they were awfully busy and I didn't like to bother them. So instead I went to the nearest big hotel and told the girl in reception what I wanted, and why. To be honest, I played the 'poor little boy in a wheelchair' bit good and hard, and the girl was sympathetic.

'I'll have a word with the manager,' she said, which I thought was a lot of fuss for a plastic container. I'd seen one in their bins, all I needed was permission to take it. But she had her reasons, and after she'd explained things on the phone, a man in a smart cream-coloured suit came into the lobby, carrying a greenish and rather mucky glass tank.

'We had it in the lounge once,' he explained, 'but now we've got a pool and fountain. I've been meaning to give it to a jumble sale, but you can have it.'

He even carried it down to the beach for me, and stopped to chat. It turned out when he wasn't hotel managering, he was a beachcombing naturalist, and Andy was really excited about some of the things the manager said he'd found, especially after a big storm. Talk about kindred spirits! Andy, this manager and Burt were linked up on their own wavelength, and after a bit they went off down the beach, the manager pushing Burt in his wheelchair and even carrying him over rocks to look into pools.

'How do you do it?' Mr Kersey asked me, grinning. 'You vanish for five minutes, and come back with a man and a free aquarium.'

'Scrounger's instinct, I suppose,' I said lightly, 'Luck.'

Or a little miracle from a kind God who was interested in little things. The thought flickered in my brain then was forgotten, as Stella asked me to take her hunting shells.

She'd been in a bit of a funny mood all morning, very edgy. Earlier, a lady had stopped to speak to Mrs Kersey, and had bought us all ice-creams. I thought that was nice of her, but Stella had a hard, angry look on her face when the lady was gone, and wouldn't eat hers (Burt and Andy shared it).

'I hate always getting pity and charity!' she blurted out, close to tears. 'I wish I could be the doer and the giver, just once! If I get into the Foot and Mouth Artists and make money selling paintings, I want to use lots of it to feed starving children in the Third World so people will see some of us disabled don't want just to take all the time!'

I didn't quite know what to say, which is rare for me.

'It's not pity,' Mr Kersey said gently. 'Sometimes, it's a kind of thank-offering. That lady probably has fit, able-bodied children of her own and is so grateful for them, she wants to help someone who hasn't been so lucky. Even in a little way.'

Stella didn't say anything more, but for me her words put a damper on the day. I was glad, though, I'd made up the kind of story I had. I told the first episode to them in the minibus going back, and saw her eyes light up at the idea of the handicapped Princess having to be the sensible, strong one (mentally strong, that it). Actually, the Princess wasn't as handicapped as Stella, she could just walk with calipers and sticks, but the principle was the same. For the boys' sake I'd made the Prince a bit less drippy, too, than I'd first intended, turning him into one of those people who can be quite good in the face of real danger, but who keep scaring themselves with their own imagination and are afraid to make a decision in case it turns out to be the wrong one. I left them with a real nail-biting situation, trapped in a cave, with a giant crab outside ready to get them if they came out, and the tide flowing in to drown them if they didn't. I was pretty pleased with it, and really thrilled when I heard Mr Kersey commenting to his wife:

'Every child who's good at English thinks they'll be a writer, but I do believe Daffy could be one who actually makes it.'

Needless to say, that dispelled the last bits of my gloom, and I went home on Cloud Nine!

CHAPTER 5

KEEPING AFLOAT

On Saturday everyone was going on an outing and tea, organized by the WI. Except me. I'd been invited to go, but I was really desperate now to get on with my raft. Podge had also gone on the outing, so after I'd delivered the stuff for Podge's mum, I began to work on it. I'd finally decided to make a little one, just big enough for me, and to make it look like the primitive reed sailing canoes I had in one of my books. I cut lots of inner tubes of different sizes in half and filled each of them with broken-up bits of polystyrene, then sealed the tops with plastic freezer bags held on with rubber wetsuit repair tape. Then I stuck them all together, with rubber glue and more tape, into a long canoe shape. The end result looked good and floated nicely, though I couldn't call it exactly stable! After I'd tested it, I hid it in our shed and went to a bit of common land where there's masses of bamboo and cut armfuls of the stuff, to tie round the canoe, weaving it in and out of the tape where there was a dip between tubes, until the whole thing looked as if it was made of reeds.

That took me all day, and I still wanted to give it a sail and a rudder, although I'd probably do more paddling than sailing. With the sort of sail I could make, I'd only be able to sail on a run – but it would look pretty. The trouble would be stepping the mast. I decided to glue a bicycle handlebar grip to the bottom and stick a broomstick on it. That would make a mast I could easily take down. To keep it up when it was supposed to be up, I'd rig string stays to the bows and sides.

I was almost satisfied that it would work. My only fear was that the thing would be too frail to survive the ramming, rotten egg fighting rough stuff at the start of the race. Still, the Best Dressed Raft judging was done before the race started, and everyone was decent enough not to use their ammunition, or attack you, until it was over, so even if I got sunk in five minutes after the race itself began, I could still win a prize.

Mum was quite impressed, but said I should have put some sort of netting round the inner tubes first, because if they got torn, I'd have a lifetime job clearing up all the polystyrene bits which would go floating down the creek!

I decided the whole idea had to be kept a deadly secret (even from the Corsairs, no matter how much they teased me), in case someone copied it. I didn't even tell Podge or Andy what I'd done.

That evening, for the first time all week, I actually watched the telly for a whole hour. I don't know why people are always saying kids watch too much television – I never seem to have the time. But there wasn't much worth watching, so after Doctor Who I went up to my room and read some of the New Testament in my Good News Bible, determined not to look ignorant when I went to Junior Church. To my surprise, I got so enthralled I had actually read right through Matthew's Gospel when Mum yelled up the stairs that it was time I put my light out and went to sleep.

On Sunday, I was off duty again. The kids were being

taken to join their pals in Red Cross House, and were going to a hospital service, then staying for lunch. I kept my promise and went along to Junior Church. To be honest, I was curious, but a bit nervous of my reception. Not that I showed it! The big pride of my life is never to show that I'm frightened. People think I'm brave, but really I'm just good at pretending.

While I'd been reading my Bible on Saturday night, a sneaking liking for Jesus got hold of me. And he'd been *human*. That was what really struck me. If he'd been the sort of serene Son of God who knew it would all come right in the end, dying on the cross wouldn't have meant nearly so much. But he'd not been immune to hurt and fear and pain. He'd been *real*.

I decided if I'd been around when he was alive, I'd probably have argued with him, but I never could have ignored him. And I had a nasty feeling that I'd have ended up following him, all the way.

My favourite heroes are brave, strong but gentle, full of compassion and humour. Jesus was all that. But he'd died ages and ages ago. The Bible said he'd died for me. But I didn't like that. I hadn't asked him to! If he had, it put me under an obligation. A bit like the medieval knights. If someone spared your life, let alone died for you, you were honour-bound not to escape, or fight against them or their cause. You didn't really own your life any more, it was theirs.

But if I owed my life to Jesus, and had to give it back to him, what would he want to do with it? It was exciting in a way that belonging to Jesus could somehow release a new kind of person inside me, the sort of person I'd never have dreamed I could be in a million years. He'd done it so often for people in the New Testament. The whole thing was like a series of adventure stories. It obviously hadn't been boring or wishy-washy being a Christian then, so maybe it was just as exciting now!

All these thoughts had been whizzing round in my mind so I got to Junior Church dying to talk to Andy.

When he saw me, he said, 'I'm really glad you've come, Fran.'

'Well, I promised,' I said. 'And don't laugh, but I've been reading the Bible. Mum gave me one. It's really good.'

There was so much I wanted to talk about, but there wasn't time. People were hurrying in for the service, and I followed Andy, feeling a bit nervous. The service started with everyone in the church, then we went out to our own groups. I must admit I'd expected school assembly-type hymns and prayers but we started with 'Morning Has Broken', which I love. We had some prayers and then a couple of choruses which I didn't know but soon picked up, and a brief story mainly for the littlest kids. Then everyone in Sunday School and Junior Church filed out.

I'd hoped to be with Andy – but I was put in a group of all girls, including Jane, Sarah and Rachel. Sarah must have been in a good mood, because she made a point of being nice to me, showing me where the toilet was, and things like that. It was all very formal – no sitting at desks or anything. We just clustered round a table, with a girl in her twenties who I knew by sight – Sue Maitland – leading us. She was in a T-shirt and jeans, just like me, and there was no way I could label her Sunday School Teacher. In fact, I missed the first bit of what she was saying because I was too busy thinking about how easily I labelled people and things, and how stupid it was, because once I'd given something a bad label, I just switched off. For ages I'd pooh-poohed the idea of Junior Church and the church because I'd stuck a label saying BORING on them, and never bothered to find out if it was true.

But I hadn't been bored at all so far, and as I began to really listen to what Sue was saying and join in the discussion, I realized that it was interesting. I can't remember exactly what started off the discussion – I think it was something in the Psalms. But the thing that came over was sharing everything with God, all your feelings, your hassles, your hopes, fears and dreams. That he was interested in every little bit of your life, and you didn't have to feel anything was too unimportant to bother him with. Not only that, but he could share the good times with us. I had a brief and glorious picture of Jesus invisibly present on the Enterprise dinghy as we went sailing across the finish line ahead of the field – really enjoying himself, sharing my enjoyment.

It was great! I can't explain it, but that first Junior Church session somehow really brought 'religion' out of a little box in a dusty corner of my mind and let it come alive.

Sue encouraged us to write our own sharings with God, our own psalm, I suppose, which was right up my street. One way and another, I was really disappointed when she looked at her watch and said:

'OK, it's time to go over for coffee.'

I couldn't stay long, because Podge and I were racing that afternoon, but I did want to have a word with Andy. He was eager to find out how I'd got on, so I told him it had been really interesting, and let him read my psalm. He liked it.

'Tell you what,' he said, 'we should do a book. I'll take photos of beautiful places and things, and you can write the words to go with them.'

I could feel myself taking off for Cloud Nine again

– to have my name on the cover of a real book is the ambition of my life. And Andy's photos are fantastic. Then Alan, the Olympic swimming hope of Truro, came up to me and said something that really brought me down to earth with a bump.

'You're seeing Podge this afternoon, aren't you?' he asked casually. 'Could you ask her if she would help my Mum with the Carnival dance? She needs someone to help with the refreshments, and I know Podge is free because I sounded her out.'

'But I thought you were going to ask her to the dance itself!' I blurted out, horrified. I knew Podge was actually making a dress!

Alan looked surprised.

'Oh, Podge isn't exactly the dance type,' he told me, grinning (great insensitive twit!). 'She's good fun and a good swimmer, and I quite like her, but . . .'

His shrug said it all. Podge was nice, but she was fat. She belonged in the kitchen, not on the dance floor. I suppose Alan was old enough to think it was important to be seen with a slim, pretty girl. But I knew Podge was going to be horribly hurt. When Alan had gone, I turned to Andy.

'She's making a dress!' I wailed. 'When he was fishing to see if she was free that evening, of course she thought . . . I mean, she's been friendly with him for a bit at the swimming club so you can't blame her for thinking . . . Oh, I could *kill* him! You know Podge. She'll help in the kitchens, if she's asked, but she'll die a bit inside. Could you take her, and I'll help in the kitchens?'

'It wouldn't work, Fran,' Andy said softly, shaking his head. 'She'd smell a rat. Anyway, it's Alan she really wants to go with, I can't afford tickets and, most important, I can't pretend to like Podge more than I like you.'

He paused after that smashing compliment, then said, 'I'll have a word with Alan. Perhaps he doesn't understand how girls think. I'm sure he doesn't realize how hurt Podge would be. People don't, because she's always laughing and joking. So don't say anything to her yet.'

'OK,' I promised, relieved. Then I had to dash, if I was going to make it home for my snack lunch, change into my 'slop kit' and get down to the sailing club in time.

It was a perfect day for racing, sunny, with about a Force 4. Strong enough to be exciting, but not really hard work. A lot of Enterprises race and competition is fierce, but Podge and I love it. We were both at the club much too early, then had to wait until the Masons arrived before we could rig. We'd both already signed the boats and crew details in, and written the course on the backs of our hands with biro. Sarah was there, too, competing with the other Topper sailors – but she's really the only one of the Corsair Toppers good enough to race, though Carolyn and Peter also compete in the Mirror class on Sundays. It's quite a long drag down the beach, so I gave Sarah a hand with her Topper and we talked for a bit about the kids.

'Stella's marvellous, isn't she?' she said, then added wistfully, 'I wish I could help with them, like you do.'

'You could join our rota. I'm sure Mr Kersey would be glad to have you,' I told her, even though I must admit I didn't particularly want her around. 'The kids have still got a week here.'

'I can't,' she said. 'I promised the Corsairs racing every day. And if I don't, Carolyn will say it's because I'm scared she and Peter will beat me. She's got really bitchy lately.'

I understood. Carolyn's supposed to be Sarah's best friend, but she'd like to lead the Corsairs and she often gets sneaky little digs in. I'm glad Podge isn't like that. It made me wonder if Sarah would always be nicer, if she had nicer friends, but with the race just about to start, I didn't have much time for wondering.

For me, it was a super race. Mr Mason and I came in second. But Mrs Mason and Podge had bad luck. They were leading when a sudden gust hit them, right at the gybe mark. They capsized, and though they righted Catweazle and caught up quite a bit, it wasn't enough. They came in about tenth. Mrs Mason was disappointed.

'I'd like one of us to win the cup before we leave,' she said to her husband, 'but it looks as if it'll have to be you.'

Leave?

Podge and I stared at each other, and Mr Mason suddenly realized we didn't know.

'Sorry,' he said, 'I've just got a transfer to my firm's branch in Canterbury. We'll be moving in October.'

'Oh. We'll miss you . . .'

'Yes,' Podge agreed miserably. 'It's been great sailing with you.'

'Oh, we'll still be around until the end of the series,' Mr Mason explained, but we knew that after that our sailing was up the spout. You had to have wet suits to take part in the winter series – and come the summer, when Podge and I (who can't afford wet suits!) could sail again, everyone would be fixed up with the crews they'd had over the winter. I felt pretty low, because I enjoy sailing, but I've got a load of other interests, so I knew I'd survive. But sailing is so very important to Podge, she was really having to fight to hold back the tears, and when we walked home, she wouldn't even

come in and have some of my Mum's chocolate cake, which shows how low she was feeling. I bet she went home, hid in her room and cried her eyes out.

And of course, I couldn't help thinking how much more awful she'd feel when she knew Alan didn't want to take her to the dance either. She'd think nobody loved her at all!

Mum took one look at my face as I dragged in, and said, 'Bad race?'

I didn't mention Podge. I just said, 'No, bad news. The Masons are moving.'

'Well, I've more bads news, I'm afraid,' Mum murmured. 'I suspect I'm going to be very unpopular with Podge, and probably with you, for interfering.'

'What do you mean?' I asked. The signs of Serious Talk were all there – she'd even got my tea ready, and Dad had come in from the garden.

Mum told me in a rush.

'Podge's Mum came round this afternoon. She's not happy at the idea of Podge going to this dance with Alan. I agreed I thought at fourteen-and-a-half Podge was too young for dates with one boy, and that I wouldn't want you to go on serious dates, even with Andy, until you were about sixteen, though I'm delighted of course for you to go around in a group of youngsters. Now I know a lot of kids date very young but . . .'

She waffled on, trying to say her piece before I exploded, explaining how she thought youngsters ran a risk of getting into emotional situations they were too immature to handle. Dad chipped in about enjoying a carefree childhood while you had the chance, and how he and Mum would take me to the right kind of dances with them, and invite Andy as my partner. But discos and heavy dates were out. Mum said she would even take me to a make-up adviser in a Truro beauty salon and have my hair styled, too, but she didn't think Podge or I should be allowed to rush headlong into growing up the wrong way.

To be honest, I let the lecture wash over me. I didn't want a big romantic scene anyway. Andy was my boy friend not my Boyfriend. So I wasn't upset, just delighted! Only one thought stuck firmly in my mnd – Podge *wouldn't be allowed to go to the dance!* She'd argue, but she wouldn't disobey. Being Podge, she'd probably ring Alan and tell him, if he wanted to ask her to the dance, forget it, she wasn't allowed to go. And she'd never need to know, unless he put his foot in it, that he hadn't meant to ask her anyway. End of problem!

'Mum, Dad, I love you!' I said impulsively, hugging Mum. I suppose they'd expected fireworks, because they just sat there, looking stunned.

'I can't explain,' I told them, 'but I think you've just solved a problem and done Podge a big favour. And I don't want heavy dates with Andy anyway. I'll only get furious if you start looking at us sideways any time we go off anywhere together. Because we're just friends.'

Mum and Dad exchanged glances, then Dad smiled.

'It's not an easy world to be a daughter's parent in,' he said. 'I just hope Podge isn't too upset. We did suggest her Mum and Dad took her.'

'And I suggested she came with you and Stella to learn how to turn yourselves into elegant young ladies,' Mum said. *'Monday's Child* are doing teen sessions all next week.'

Monday's Child is a hairdressers really, but they do a bit of make-up and fashion advice on the side.

'Oh, I can't be bothered,' I said lightly, 'but I know Stella would like it. She's ever so pretty. It seems an awful shame that when she's older, her handicap will probably put boys off. And yet I don't know – Mike

Spargo seemed to get on pretty well with her.'

'It wouldn't hurt you to learn how to look nice for special occasions,' Dad argued, and I flashed back:

'Now who wants me to grow up before my time? I happen to like slopping around, and I don't care a bit what I look like.'

They gave up then, but at 6 p.m. Jane came round. Mum was going to evening service and Jane was walking down with her. They both sing in the choir. I've always teased Jane about her Sunday best (and about going to two services on Sunday!) but this time I caught sight of us side by side in our big hall mirror. And it made me think.

There was Jane, who's small and delicate, her shining hair falling neatly, a straw summer hat on, and one of those simple lineny dresses that I hate because you have to iron them. And a linen jacket, ditto. Plus *clean* white sandals.

And there was me, radiantly beautiful in a faded Windsurfer T-shirt, cut-off, frayed jeans with a towelling patch sewn across the backside for non-slip sailing, *filthy* plimsols and my long, straggly hair thick with sea salt.

So what did it matter? I was only thirteen and I didn't want to be Miss World. But it niggled somehow.

CHAPTER 6

HOW TO BECOME A
HEROINE

Monday, I was on duty with John and Andy. Dave would be with us too, just for the afternoon. Because it was fine, and natural history is Andy's thing, in the morning we went to a farm where the farmer, a real bird fanatic, had made his own little reserve, with a hide accessible to wheelchairs. We didn't stay long. Burt was keen, but Anna got bored with just watching since there wasn't a pony in sight! As I wheeled her back to the minibus, Stella said softly:

'I'm afraid of when we go back. It's always boring in the ward, or usually, anyway. They never minded before, but now they know there's more to living, they even know how to be bored. It's easier for me because I go out to school, and the school has outside activities too . . .'

She paused, and her eyes were suddenly tear-bright and angry.

'Just because they can't do much, and maybe they're not very bright, people don't think it matters! I bet if I couldn't speak, I'd be left to vegetate too! Being able to communicate must be the most important thing in the whole world . . .'

Then she sighed. 'Sorry,' she muttered, 'I got carried away.'

As if it was anything to apologise for! I couldn't quite

understand how she felt, because I'd never had a problem that way. But I did try to imagine it, having a brilliant mind but not being able to speak, write or even signal to make people understand what I needed or felt. It was a nasty thought. Much worse than being stuck in a foreign country where you didn't know the language – at least you could point and mime. And because you couldn't communicate, people would think you were daft. They'd not even bother to talk to you or read to you. And I couldn't help wondering if there were children like that, trapped in a world of helpless frustration.

'You're subdued, Daffy,' Mr Kersey said to me as we had our picnic lunch, and I told him what I was thinking. He nodded.

'We're all learning a lot from these kids,' he agreed, 'and the hardest thing to face is that maybe they're just the tip of the iceberg. I wonder what happens to badly handicapped kids in the Third World? I suppose they're just left to die, in most cases.'

Stella overheard. In a terrible, cold little voice she said softly, 'Some people think *we* should. A lady actually said in my hearing once that it would be kinder to have let us die. Sometimes when I'm really miserable I think she was right, then life gives me something nice and I think, no, I want to live, I've got a right to live – maybe I've even got a *purpose* to live for. What right has anyone got to scrap me?'

After that, I felt all churned up inside and not even visiting the seal sanctuary helped. The seals were adorable, especially the young ones, and I'd have loved to swim with them. But I kept on thinking how baby seals were killed to make fur coats, and how cruel and uncaring people were – killing animals, just for fun or fashion, killing other people, or just letting them die. I wasn't so special myself, I knew. I didn't give all my pocket money to feeding the hungry or anything, but I did do a bit, even if it was only to help collect jumble for an Oxfam sale to help starving children. And I wanted the world to change. I wanted desperately to do something, even if I didn't know what.

Luckily, though, when we got back to the Kerseys, something happened that cheered me up and reassured me people were nice, after all. As the postman hadn't come before we left, Mr Kersey opened his mail as we ate tea. Suddenly he let out a delighted whoop and waved a letter at us.

'You know that man who brought us the aquarium at Perranporth?' he said. 'Well, apparently he wasn't just the manager, he was the owner's son and partner. They want to discuss the possibility of having either you kids or some others from your hospital for a week's free holiday at the beginning of next season. They say they can put up six children, plus helpers and staff, in their ground level chalet annexe.'

'Fantastic!' John said, and Andy beamed at me.

'All because you went to scrounge a plastic ice-cream tub', he whispered. 'Do you think if we went to a different seaside town each day and tried to scrounge plastic tubs from the most hopeful looking hotels . . . ?'

I giggled, but it was a lovely thing to happen, a starting point for the things we wanted to arrange for the kids in the future. I went home loving the whole generous, big-hearted human race again! With the possible exception of Alan.

As we walked home from the Kerseys, Andy said he'd managed to catch Alan, but not only had he refused to take Podge, he'd actually asked another girl from her school.

'Luckily, Podge rang when I was there,' he said, 'and

told him she wasn't going to go. I kicked him so he would remember to sound disappointed. Sorry I didn't get the chance to tell you before, but there was always someone else around.'

'That's OK,' I said. 'I think my Mum persuaded her Mum that she shouldn't date yet. I only hope she doesn't hold it against me, that she's been stopped from going.'

'Not Podge,' Andy replied, 'she's not the type.'

I hoped he was right. That dance had mattered quite a lot to Podge.

I was 'off duty' next day, but I'd promised to go in just for the first hour, to help get the kids ready to go out. I called for Podge, with my heart in my mouth, but though she was a bit quiet she didn't seem cross with me or my mum. In fact, she didn't even mention the dance and I didn't dare, just in case I put my foot in it. It was Stella who asked, in the end, how her dress was getting on. She's quite romantic, Stella. I suppose in the ward the nurses talk about their boyfriends quite a lot. Most of the hospital books Mum sometimes gets from the library have lots more romance than medicine!

'Is it finished yet?' she asked eagerly. 'Can we see it? I've got a pendant you could borrow to go with it – a golden one, with a tiger's eye.'

A tight look came into Podge's face. I can't describe it easily, she sort of stiffened, a bit like a cat when a dog comes too near.

'Oh, I've finished it,' she said, too casually, 'but I've decided not to go anyway.'

'Not to go?' Stella was appalled, and she didn't know Podge well enough to realize she didn't want to answer any questions. 'Why not? Have you and Alan quarrelled?'

'Was it your Mum?' I asked guiltily. 'Mine gave me a lecture on being Too Young to Date and apparently she'd said much the same to your Mum about you.'

'Mum did say that she and Dad would take me and Alan, rather than us going on our own,' Podge admitted, 'if I really wanted to go. But I told her I'd already decided not to – I'd just gone off the idea. Who wants to go dancing anyway?'

Now I was really confused. She'd have given her eye teeth to go before! The only thing I could think of was that Alan had somehow let on he'd not meant to take her – maybe Angela, the girl he had asked, had told Podge or something. In which case I decided I would personally kick her into the creek!

Stella wouldn't give up.

'Oh, but it would be so lovely!' she wailed. 'I was relying on you to tell us all about it. Swirling round in long dresses while the band played ... Nurse Helen took me to her engagement dance in April, it was beautiful! Do change your mind – if it's just that you don't know how to do the old-fashioned dances, I can teach you. I can't show you the steps, obviously, but I know them and I can tell you ...'

How I wished she'd give over! I made eye signals at her, but she wasn't looking at me, all her attention was on Podge. I could see Podge was getting more and more uptight. She'd have told anyone else to belt up, but didn't have the heart to be rude to Stella. I had a wild try at saving the situation.

'Oh, I think Podge is right not to go,' I argued. 'She needs her sleep if she's to win the water sports. We have no end of dances she can go to, but the water sports are only once a year. And we've got to show those Corsairs by winning a cup or two.'

Then I added in sudden inspiration:

'Major Vickers is taking Miss Franklin so she can tell you all about it. Hey — I wonder if there's a love story cooking there? He's a widower, and the right age.'

Poor old Major Vickers! I knew jolly well that he's been taking Miss Franklin to dances for years, for no better reason that that they both like ballroom dancing! But it was enough to set Stella off on a new scent, and Podge gave me a thankful look. Soon, it was all forgotten anyway, as they set off and I ran home to get on with my raft.

I'd already tie-dyed an old sheet — now I made part of it into a big, bright sail, fixed to two bits of dowel rod. Then I tied a makeshift rudder to the raft. I was all set to fit the sail to the mast, when Mum asked me to take a cake she'd made for a Guess the Weight competition down to Mr Trevanson. Going down to his shop would probably mean seeing the Corsairs, which didn't please me much, so I moaned. I was afraid I might let on about the raft if they started teasing me – that it was done, and what it was like. Then someone might copy me. But Mum was adamant.

'Just take no notice of them,' she said, putting the enormous cake into a tin and giving it to me. 'Anyway, you'll show them on the day.'

'Not if I don't get my sail done properly!' I grumbled. But I knew arguing wouldn't get me very far, so I just decided to get the errand over with as quickly as I could.

Sure enough, the Corsairs were all there on the jetty and worse luck, Mr Trevanson was with them, so I couldn't just sneak unnoticed into his shop and dump the cake. But they didn't pay me a bit of attention: they were all arguing like fury. Mr Williams, Carolyn's dad, was there, and Carolyn was crying. Bewildered, I listened for a bit. I couldn't make out what the trouble was, until Carolyn howled:

'I did tie her up properly! I know I did! Someone else must have loosed her!'

Then she glared at Sarah, and Sarah glared back.

'Well, I didn't, so there,' she said fiercely.

Carolyn took no notice. 'Just because we beat you hollow yesterday, I bet you thought you'd nobble us!' she spat, which was a really rotten thing to say. Sarah may get up my nose sometimes, but she's not that kind of nasty cheat. And sailing people just don't untie other people's boats.

'I did not untie your beastly Mirror!' she exploded, white with fury.

'Well, it didn't untie itself and we'd better find it,' Mr Williams said. By then, of course, I'd got the picture, and I thought I'd better say something, because I felt sorry for Sarah and even for Carolyn. I don't like them, but it's rotten to lose your boat, and I guessed Carolyn was really desperate not to upset her dad. You know how people gossip in a village. Everyone said, even in front of us kids, how the Williams had fought non-stop since he came back from France and nobody would be surprised if he left his wife, the way she'd been behaving. And I supposed Carolyn loved her Dad. I mean, I love mine, I'd hate him to leave us. So she wouldn't want him to be angry with her, too. But it was also rotten for poor Sarah, knowing her supposed best friend could believe she would do something so mean and nasty.

So I said something which wasn't quite a lie, though not exactly true.

'It was probably nicked,' I suggested. 'Some of the holiday-makers' kids have been "borrowing" dinghies, mucking about in them, and abandoning them. It's happened over at St Just and Percueil.'

They all turned to me, and Mr Trevanson nodded.

'That makes more sense,' he agreed. 'If she'd just drifted, she'd not have gone far. And with so many Mirrors around, nobody would have really registered a strange kid in yours. I'll take my boat out and look. What's her number?'

Carolyn, silly twit, couldn't remember, but Peter told him.

'We can search from our dinghies,' Sarah suggested. She gave me a feeble smile of thanks, but wouldn't look at Carolyn.

'I'll drive over the ferry,' Mr Williams added. 'Check out the other side of the river.'

I said I'd scramble round the banks, and search down as far as the King Harry ferry, if the ones in boats covered the upper bit of Carrick Roads and the lower end of the Creek. So we split up.

Now, to be honest, I didn't expect to find anything, but it was fun scrambling round to the King Harry. At high tide, it's a bit dodgy because there are steep bits, rocks and slippery woodland paths. But it's very pretty, and you can often see herons. Best of all, this time, if I accidentally trespassed on anyone's private property, I'd have a good excuse. So I dumped the cake in the shop and set off, pretending to be the guard on a top-secret base.

From time to time I'd switch to being Robinson Crusoe and stand, shading my eyes, staring out to sea. After all, I wasn't a Corsair so I couldn't really feel that upset and worried about Carolyn's boat. I saw the dinghies moving out – two Toppers heading for Mylor, the Tutor 10 and one Topper cutting over to St Just. Jason had been detailed to go up the creek because it was a bit windy and rough in the Roads for his little Optimist. Mr Trevanson was chugging up towards

Falmouth. Then I turned the point and lost sight of them all.

It was lovely and peaceful. Normally, there's lots of boats about, but everyone seemed to be having a siesta. All alone, a fearless guard, I scrambled among the bushes. It was quite a drop to the water. About twenty feet, I suppose, but I could easily imagine a sheer, 300 foot cliff. A big, rusty old buoy became the conning tower of an enemy submarine, and I opened fire at the saboteurs with my machine gun.

Then I saw him.

That's how easy it is to become a heroine. I saw the inverted Mirror first. Then I saw him. They just happened to be where only someone standing where I was, or on the bank opposite, or approaching from downriver, could see them. The boy was swimming feebly a few yards offshore. He went under, and when he came up, he floated limply, face down in the water.

Suddenly, I wasn't pretending any more. Cold as ice inside and horribly frightened, I started to scramble down the bank, slipped, and fell heavily, landing on my bottom. A pain gripped me like an iron corset from my hips to my chest and I knew I'd done something to hurt myself. But there wasn't time to worry. I got up, scrambled painfully over the last rock, and slid into the water. Although I wasn't old enough to take my Bronze, Dad had taught me lifesaving, and even though it hurt, it was easy for me to turn the boy right way up and tow him the short distance in. He was only a kid.

But he wasn't breathing.

I prayed then, and cried, but even as my mind was going round in a panic, my fingers cleared his mouth out. I didn't try to get him out of the water. As soon as I could stand in my depth, I tilted his head back, pinched his nose and started mouth to mouth resuscitation.

Three quick, short puffs then ... in – watch chest rise – breathe myself, counting 1, 2, 3, 4, 5 – blow more air in.

I was trembling all over, I felt woozy, and wanted to faint. My back and chest still hurt, and I knew I must have sprained or broken something. But miraculously, the kid's lips were no longer a horrid bluish colour. My air was going in.

'Jesus,' I prayed silently, from my heart, 'I don't deserve any favours, because I've never believed in you properly, but that's not his fault, please bring him back to life, please.'

Then I heard the outboard motor. Between breaths, I screamed for help, and a minute later a strong, calm, mercifully grown-up voice said:

'OK my bird. We'll take over.'

They were two fishermen, in a big dinghy, and I've never been so glad to see anybody in my whole life. One grabbed the kid and bundled him into the boat, the other immediately took over resuscitation. Then the first one helped me in. I yelped.

'You hurt?' he asked, and I told him how I'd fallen down the bank, trying to reach the boy. Then I began to cry in earnest. I just couldn't help it. It's very nice to imagine yourself in thrilling situations, but another thing to be actually in them – then it's for real, and you don't know if the ending is going to be happy.

Grim-faced, the man turned the throttle up to full, and we sped back to Peveran jetty, bouncing over the waves. Every bounce hurt. But just as we got there, the kid started breathing for himself, made a whimpering noise, and was sick.

'Thank God!' we said in unison.

After that, things happened in a blur. A local sailor who I knew by sight but not name bundled us into his car and rushed us to Out-patients at the local hospital. The boy was whisked away somewhere and a woman in white took all my personal details and said she'd ring Mum. Then I was taken to X-ray in a wheelchair after a doctor had examined me. I stood awkwardly and uncomfortably in front of the machine, and when the plates were ready, the doctor looked at them and whistled.

'Orthopaedic ward for you, young lady,' she said.

'Oh, no!' I wailed. 'I can't stay in. I've got a raft to finish, and I've got to practise before Saturday!'

'You won't be making or racing rafts for a bit,' she warned. 'You're going to have to take life nice and easy. You've crushed a vertebra – one of the bones in your spine – and your back's as crooked as a dog's hind leg.'

I just gawped at her, unable to believe it. I'd always thought if you broke your back, you ended up paralysed.

'No spinal cord injury,' she explained. 'You're one very lucky girl.'

Then I was wheeled back to the main Out-patients Department. Mum, who'd arrived by then, was looking white as a sheet. She kissed me.

'I'm proud of you,' she said, and in such a way that it meant more than a hundred flattering words. Then the doctor explained things.

'Fortunately, it seems to be a very stable crush fracture. As she's already walked, swum, travelled in a boat and a car with it, I see no point in deciding now to encase her in plaster, confine her to bed or in fact interfere with nature in any way.'

Relief number one, I thought. Podge had once

broken her arm, and she said the itching inside the plaster drove her crazy.

'However,' the doctor added, 'we'll keep her under observation for a couple of days, because of the twisting of her spine – though I'm almost sure it will literally straighten itself out.'

'Please let me go home by Saturday,' I begged, 'so I can at least watch the Regatta and the Carnival.'

'We'll do our best,' she promised. Then I asked about the kid. (I'm ashamed to say, it was a bit of an after-thought!)

'He'll be OK,' the doctor reassured me. 'It's shock mainly, now. But you saved his life.'

That made me feel very small, very grateful and curiously humble. Because it was God really – I'd just been in the right place at the right time, and somehow I'd been able to do the right things. But the more I thought about it, the more I felt sure I hadn't been alone. I didn't quite understand how I felt, let alone how to put it into words, so I just blushed and asked if it had been Carolyn's Mirror, and if it was OK. Of course, the doctor hadn't a clue. Then I was carted off to the orthopaedic ward. Luckily, Mum had been told to bring overnight things for me, just in case. Although I didn't much fancy having to try to sleep in a place like a big, noisy dormitory, I was quite curious – and to be honest, though I pretended I didn't really need to stay in bed or a chair, I hurt so much I was secretly glad to be fussed over. They asked me if I needed anything for the pain, but it wasn't agony or anything like that, just a determined sort of ache.

A kind Sister suggested I must be pretty shaken up, and a little sleep would probably do me good, so I went to bed. Mum vanished with a promise to return at visiting time, and to my surprise I fell asleep at once.

CHAPTER 7

MIRROR, MIRROR

I woke just before dinner-time, feeling stiff and sore, and needing to go to the loo. I walked there with a dear little old lady who'd just had a hip operation, and she had to slow down for me! But I was feeling bright otherwise, and very hungry. Dinner was sausage, chips and peas – and I even allowed myself some chips. (Unlike Podge, I always watch my figure!)

Lots of things had been delivered for me. There were flowers from Mr and Mrs Kersey, and a note dictated by the kids, saying they would visit me if I stayed in long enough. Mr and Mrs MacKay, the Masons and Mr Trevanson had all sent fruit and the fishermen had sent a half bottle of real champagne with a note saying 'Only the best for a heroine!' (Worse luck, sister wouldn't let me drink it.) There was a huge bouquet from a Mr and Mrs James, who turned out to be the parents of the boy I'd rescued. Andy had brought a bunch of flowers. He'd come in, and had been allowed into the ward, but he'd just left the flowers and crept away because I was asleep. Silly twit should have woken me – I'd have liked to see him!

Podge, who'd been told she could come in and see me the next day if I was still there, sent a box of home-made fudge and a note saying I was a lucky beast and nobody ever tried to drown when she was around.

John, Jane and Dave all signed a 'Get Well' card (Dave can write his name) and to my surprise I got a letter from Sarah which answered a lot of my questions. It said:

'Well done, and thanks for sticking up for me. I didn't untie Carolyn's Mirror. Jason found it by the bridge, moored up. You know Angela who hires a Mirror from Mr Curnow? Well, she tied the Mirror to our jetty, and rang Mr Curnow to say she'd have to leave it there because she wasn't well. Mr Curnow sent Ben to get it, and he picked up Carolyn's by mistake.' (That I could well believe. At school, we call Ben The Brain, because he wants to be an inventor. He's brilliant, but the most absent-minded boy I have *ever* met!)

The letter continued, 'Then instead of sailing it back home straight away, he went down the creek to visit one of his mates. We might have guessed, seeing the other Mirror there, that someone had taken Carolyn's by mistake, but I suppose we were all too het up. Carolyn and Peter said sorry to me. I'm sorry I've been beastly to you sometimes. I think you were very brave.'

Well – from Sarah, that was quite something!

Dad fitted the rest of the pieces of the story together, when he came at visiting time, bringing me a pack of super second-hand books, and another one on loan from Miss Franklin.

The boy, whose name was Kevin, had his own Mirror. He'd done a bit of sailing on a reservoir at home but was really only a beginner. They were staying at Penharrow Farm and Kevin had been told not to take his Mirror out that day because it was too windy. So he'd gone for a walk. Then, bored and sulking, he decided he could handle the wind and took it out even though he hadn't got his life jacket with him. But he hadn't counted on the waves, and in trying to get the boat to go about, he'd capsized. Mirrors can be beasts to right when they invert (which they often do) and he just couldn't get her up. So instead of doing the sensible thing, sitting on her and yelling for help, he'd tried to swim ashore, but he was cold, tired and a poor swimmer. Which was where I'd come in.

I realized he'd been a bit of an idiot, but I felt sorry for the kid. I'd done daft things myself, but always escaped real trouble. I said as much to Mum and Dad.

'I'm only thankful you were there and remembered what to do,' Dad said, ruffling my hair. 'And I'm some proud of you.'

'I was scared,' I admitted. 'And I prayed like mad.'

Dad nodded. 'Never be ashamed of either fear or prayers,' he said, and Mum smiled.

It was funny, because I should have been feeling brave, and strong and special, but I wasn't. I kept thinking of how frightened I'd been. And of Kevin. How it must have felt for him, and how everything had fitted together to save him. As though Somebody had been in command of the whole situation, and had put me where I was needed and given me the strength to do what I had to.

I thought how it would have been if I'd been in Kevin's place. Mum and Dad upset, hurt I couldn't be trusted; me almost killed and responsible for someone else being injured. What if I'd ended up paralysed for life? How would Kevin have felt then?

It couldn't be just chance the way things had conspired to put me in the right place at the right time to save him. One girl and a boy moor a Mirror for a brief while – another girls feels ill and moors another Mirror. A boy collects the wrong one. I volunteer to search along a particular bit of bank. If Kevin had capsized a bit earlier or a bit later, might he have drowned? If it had been someone else on that bank, someone who couldn't swim or do the kiss of life? Perhaps there was even a reason for me smashing my back, so it gave me time to lie still and think. And those fishermen coming just when I needed them . . .

All these thoughts went through my head very quickly, while Dad and Mum were telling me how the news had spread round the village; how the police had come to the farm where Mr James and his wife were staying, and rushed them to the hospital.

'We had all sorts of people calling at the shop or at home all afternoon,' Mum said, 'including a reporter from *The West Briton*, so you may make the headlines on Thursday!'

Then a man came rather shyly to join us, a kind-looking man with worried eyes. He introduced himself to me and Dad as Kevin's father – he'd already met Mum.

'Please don't be too angry with Kevin,' I said impulsively, and he smiled.

'We're not,' he assured me. 'We're too relieved to have him alive, and thanks to you. My wife's with him now, but she'd also like to come and see you later.'

'How is he?' Mum asked, and Mr James said that he was in no danger, although they were keeping him in overnight for observation, and that he was still very shaken up.

'He's shocked in more than the medical sense,' his father explained, smiling ruefully. 'He's had a sharp lesson he won't forget in a hurry. And so have we. He's just not old enough, or should I say, responsible enough, to have a boat of his own. At the moment, he says he'll never go on or near the water again, but if he changes his mind, we'll sail together as a family.'

Dad nodded. 'It's easier for kids like Daffy,' he said. 'Brought up near the sea, they learn to treat it with respect. For other children, it's just a holiday plaything – they don't realize how dangerous it can be.'

'Anyway, the Mirror's going,' Mr James told us. Then he looked at me. 'Now I know you wouldn't want a reward, young lady, but a third-hand Mirror dinghy that isn't wanted any more hardly qualifies, so if you'd like it, it's yours. I've left it with Mr Trevanson.'

I didn't know what to say. I didn't want a reward, of course – but a dinghy! Podge could use it for the Regatta, and we could share it afterwards.

'If you don't want it,' Mr James added, 'I won't sell it, I'll give it to the local Sea Scouts.'

'Oh, no,' I protested. 'They've got three Mirrors already which they hardly use, because they like canoeing better.'

'Give it a good home, then,' Mr James urged, and I gave in, accepted and thanked him very much. I also told him about Podge and the Regatta, and he was quite happy for her to sail it. 'From this moment, it's yours,' he said. 'You can let anyone you like sail it.'

Mum and Dad were both grinning happily. He must have asked Mum first, then thrown in the bit about the Sea Scouts to get me to accept. But he hadn't finished. He pulled something out of a carrier bag and put it on the bed – a bright scarlet buoyancy aid.

'Kevin should have worn it, and I know you will,' he said. Then, almost as if he was scared I'd thank him some more, he left.

'Wow!' I breathed. Mum laughed.

'I'm glad,' she said. 'You deserved it. But I'm afraid you won't do any more sailing this summer. The doctors say they'll let you swim gently in a pool after a few weeks, but no other exercise except walking, for about three months. We might even borrow a wheelchair from the Red Cross for a few days, as you'll hurt too much to walk far.'

'I don't need a wheelchair!' I protested. Then I thought again. It could be interesting to see what it really felt like being pushed around. Not that I could feel really disabled inside, because I'd know I was just pretending – just in the wheelchair for a little while. But it might give me some idea how kids like Stella must feel. So I agreed. I wasn't too pleased at the ban on doing active things, but at least Andy was still pretty much in the same position – not so badly, but off sports until September at least. And after all, I might have been paralysed for life, so I couldn't really complain. I'd got enough sense to realize how lucky I was.

'Tell Podge about the dinghy when you go home,' I begged. 'She'll be thrilled!'

They promised they would, then Mrs James came in. She actually burst into tears as she thanked me, which was horribly embarrassing, and though I tried to convince her I hadn't done anything that special, I couldn't have been more heroic in her eyes if I'd been Flash Gordon saving the Universe. I suppose the whole thing must have shaken her up so much, she couldn't think straight.

Then visiting time was over, hot drinks came round, and the ward settled down for the night. I fell asleep quickly, but woke at 1 a.m., my back hurting a lot and a very old lady crying out for someone while a nurse gently soothed her. Somewhere a machine was ticking, and another patient was snoring. Mum had brought me earplugs (sensible Mum!) but I had to get up to ease the pain in my back. It helped to sit sort of twisted in a chair, just for a minute. The old lady stopped calling and fell asleep and the nurse, seeing me, said she'd make me a hot drink.

'Better than sleeping pills,' she said, bringing a mug of hot chocolate for me. She had what I can only call a good face – gentle, open, loving. I suppose she was in her late fifties. I would have liked to talk to her, but contented myself with a whispered thanks.

The chocolate was welcome. It was strangely peaceful to sit and drink it in the blue-lit ward, while outside the town slept. Or most of it. A few night workers would be busy, a few late birds driving home after an evening out, watched by the cops in their patrol cars. Somewhere, perhaps, there were sad scenes: a mother peeping in on a sick child; a nurse watchful over a dying patient. Maybe someone was in a phone box, pills in their pocket, ringing the Samaritans. The night was a blanket of secrecy over thousands of lives. Mum says I've got a vivid imagination, and I'm glad to say she's right (all writers *have to have* vivid imaginations, don't they?). The things I read in the papers become real to me when I stop to think about them.

And I could easily imagine God watching over the whole lot, knowing not just every happening, but every thought, every feeling. I knew it deep down inside me, knew he was even totally aware of me drinking my hot chocolate. On impulse, I closed my eyes.

'Thank you for helping me today, God,' I whispered. 'Thank you for saving Kevin. Thank you for people being so nice to me. Thank you that I'm not paralysed. Please help me to help all the sad and suffering people in the world somehow.'

God and Jesus melted together in my thoughts as if I couldn't have one without the other too. I wanted to be right with them, to feel sure that they not only loved me but were pleased with me, yet I was afraid, too. For the first time ever it occurred to me that Jesus might not want me after all. I'd been so busy thinking about whether I wanted *him* – but I'd put him off so much, even fought against him, that maybe I was out of the running. Once I wouldn't have cared a bit – he didn't want me, so what? I didn't want him! But now I realized I didn't like the idea at all! I felt like I'd felt when I almost lost Andy's friendship – only worse.

Because I was scared I might start crying or something equally stupid, I reached for a book. If I lost myself in its words, I could forget my thoughts. The nearest book was the one Miss Franklin had sent, *My Left Foot* by a bloke called Christy Brown, and as I picked it up, a bookmark fluttered onto my lap. I looked at it. It was a picture of Jesus with a lantern in his hand, knocking on a door. It had no latch – so it couldn't be opened from the outside. Mum had a print of this, so I knew it – Holman Hunt's *Light of the World*. Underneath it said, 'Behold, I stand at the door and knock – if anyone hears my voice and opens the door, I will come in to him.'

I knew what it meant, and relief flooded through me. Those were Jesus' words. They meant I wasn't ever going to be shut away from him, except by my own choice. He was still knocking. I just had to make up my mind, once and for all, to open the door.

Only I couldn't quite, not then. One last little part of me wasn't ready to give in. Drowsy again, I finished up my chocolate, snuggled deep into the bed, and fell asleep.

CHAPTER 8

DAFFY ON WHEELS

All at once, it was morning. Ward routine doesn't give you much time to think – temperature, pulse, bathroom to wash. They told me I could have a bath, so I did. We have a well at home and though it's never run dry, Mum rations me to two baths a week in summer. I washed my hair, too. It was full of Carrick Roads salt.

After breakfast, I started chatting to the other patients. A lot were elderly, but there were younger ones too – a girl who'd been hurt in a car crash, and another not much older than me who'd had her knee done. But I didn't get much time for talking before I was ordered back to bed as the Consultant doctor was coming round. He examined me, tested my reflexes, asked a lot of questions, then smiled.

'I'm going to take a chance and send you home, young lady,' he said to my delight. 'But you must promise to do nothing energetic, and come in for more X-rays on Friday.'

I promised like a shot.

It was arranged for Dad and Mum to bring my clothes in at afternoon visiting time, so I didn't really think I'd see anyone else before then. Once the consultant had gone, I asked Sister if I could wander round and look at the rest of the hospital.

'Providing you use the lifts and go carefully,' she

agreed. 'You can change into your ordinary day clothes.'

So I did. But when I was actually leaving the ward, Sister had gone for a tea break or something and a nurse told me anxiously that I must go in a wheelchair, so there was no chance of me falling and injuring my back. She looked very young and had only one stripe, so I suppose she was a first year. I thought there was far more chance of my falling out of a wheelchair, which I'd never used before, than off my own two feet, but she was adamant. So an old wheelchair was dug out from somewhere, and after experimenting a bit up and down the ward, I set off.

It was surprisingly hard work, even on the level. And it was a bit like rowing – if you pulled the least bit more on one side than the other, you started to go in circles. I'd taken my purse in case I wanted anything in the League of Friends canteen and when it slipped off my lap, I bent forward instinctively to pick it up. At once my back screamed in protest and the wheelchair almost tipped me out! Shaken, I came alongside the purse instead, but that wasn't much easier, and I was grateful when somebody hurrying down the corridor picked it up for me.

'Here you are, dear. Want a push anywhere?' she asked, and I smiled.

'I'm looking for the lift,' I explained, and she took me there, with all the effortless speed of someone used to wheelchairs.

'My eldest is in one of these, only smaller,' she said in a matter of fact way. 'And I'm afraid his brother will be, before long. They've got muscular dystrophy.'

'Oh!' I gasped. 'How awful for you!' I knew as yet it couldn't be cured, at least not the severe form I'd read about. It just got worse and worse. But this incredible lady smiled.

'We've come to terms with it,' she said. 'There's still hope and we're still fighting. Now – where are you heading?'

'Nowhere special,' I admitted, 'just looking around.'

'I'm going over to the Assessment Unit. Like to come?'

'Yes, please.'

It would have taken me ages to reach the lift – she got me there in a minute. I glared at it.

'The buttons are pretty high,' I grunted, disgusted. 'I'd really have to reach up for them. I'm not used to this,' I admitted. 'I've only just injured my back. But I'm lucky – I'm able to move my legs and everything.' I twiddled my feet to prove it. 'I'm just not allowed to walk at the moment.'

The lift descended with a hiccup. I think I would have been quite frightened in there on my own, stuck in a wheelchair. I could just have reached the emergency button but what if I tipped out of the chair trying? It occurred to me that even everyday things needed quite a lot of courage if you were disabled.

'I'd just like to call in at the shop,' the lady said, interrupting my thoughts. That was useful, because I wanted to go too. While she bought a few bags of sweets, I was able to choose some chocolates for the ward staff and doctors. I couldn't reach across the counter with my money, so the lady had to pay for me and give me my change. I know it's only a little thing, but even that niggled somehow. It made me feel like a helpless little kid.

To get to the Assessment Centre, we came out and cut across the hospital grounds. I heard the place before I saw it – lots of excited shrieks! We'd had children at the Tadpole Club who'd come from there, so I knew what it was – a place where they assessed the little kids who were disabled and helped the parents and families. It seemed more like a big, successful playgroup as we went in – lots of children with their Mums, staff and helpers and masses of toys.

'My two are at a boarding special school during the week,' said the lady who'd brought me. 'So I started helping here, just one day a week. I enjoy it so much I even come during the holidays now. When I'm here, my two go and spend the day with one of their mates. I think they're glad to be free of Mum's fussing for a bit.'

Before she left me, she told me that when I went back, I should get off the road and onto the path going across to the main hospital. The road sloped steeply either side of this place, too steep for a chair, and met busy main roads at the bottom. I stayed for a bit, watching the little kids and talking to some of them, then I wheeled myself out after a bit of a fight with the door. I saw what my helper had meant about the road. How did people manage hills in wheelchairs? The rotten things don't even have gears!

By the time I got back to the main hospital my hands were quite sore, my arms tired, my back ached and I wanted to go to the loo. Naturally, I went to the nearest one marked 'Ladies' but it wasn't for ladies in wheelchairs! I'm afraid I cheated then – I left the wheelchair outside and walked in.

After only a couple of hours I was fed up with the idea of being disabled, and not anywhere near as badly disabled as Stella and the other kids! When I finally got back to the ward, Sister looked surprised to see me in the chair and laughed when I shoved it in a corner in disgust.

'I never want to be stuck in one of them again!' I growled.

She laughed and said, 'I'd like to see town planners and architects spend at least one day a year in a wheelchair,' she said, then hustled me to the lunch table.

But I can tell you – even my brief foray into the world of the disabled had opened my eyes a lot!

Mum and Dad were the first people through the doors at visiting time. They brought presents for the staff, and a case for all my stuff. Instead of taking me straight home, they drove down to the quay and parked by Mr Trevanson's shop. I was a bit surprised then I realized why. All the kids were there, some from Junior Church and all the Corsairs and the Kerseys, the Masons, and Jane's aunt. And at the head of the jetty was the pretty little Mirror I'd last seen upside down.

'As she's yours,' Dad explained, 'Podge wouldn't sail her until you'd done the launching ceremony. Mr Trevanson salvaged her and we've painted out her old name. You can choose any stick-on letters you like for the new name from Mr Trevanson's stock. And launch her with your fishermen's champagne.'

It was such a gorgeous surprise I felt like bursting into tears of sheer happiness. Luckily, I stopped myself.

'I'll call her *Lowena*,' I decided. (It's Cornish for Joy.)

Honestly, it was marvellous! The only thing we didn't have was a band. I couldn't comfortably crouch on the jetty to stick the letters on, so Podge did it for me. Then I asked her to take the helm ready to give the boat her first sail once she'd been christened. Beaming all over her face, Podge obeyed. We didn't want to scratch her bows, so Dad uncorked the champagne and I just sprayed it over the Mirror as I named her and wished good luck to all who sailed in her. Then Podge

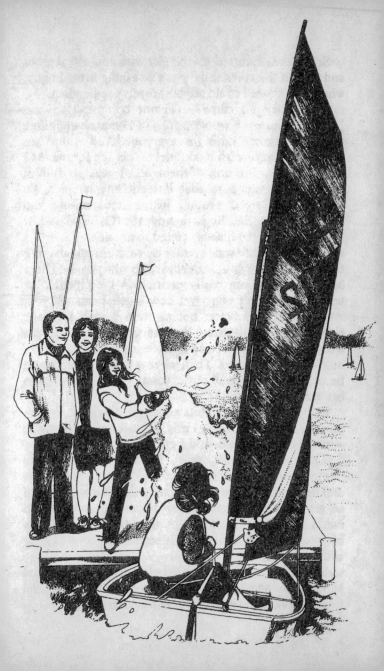

took her out, escorted by the Corsairs and a few other boats from the creek. She was a smashing little dinghy, even from shore I could see how nicely she handled.

Then they all came in again, because Dad had brought a crate – a whole *crate* – of Pomagne and there were polystyrene cups for everyone. And Anna was wheeled forward with a bouquet on her lap for me. As I thanked her, I thanked them all. I was so full of happiness, I was sure that if I got any happier, I'd burst! They stood around joking and smiling and talking about the Regatta and the Carnival, while Andy manoeuvred his way round to my side.

'What you did was great!' he said. Then, making sure nobody else could overhear, he whispered. 'There could be something really exciting in the pipeline for next year. I don't know yet how much I can tell you, and I'd certainly better not mention it with everyone else around. But after I've finished with the kids tomorrow, I'll come round and see you, OK?'

'You bet!' I agreed. Then we saw Podge coming, and he began to tell me about a young owl that had been brought to him.

Podge was thrilled to bits about the dinghy.

'And you really don't mind if I sail her until you're allowed to?' she asked, and I grinned.

'Of course I don't, twit!' I said. 'And when I'm allowed, we'll sail her together.'

Then we had to break the party up. Dad said he had to get back to the shop, and wanted to run me and Mum home first. Actually, he used that as an excuse. He wanted a private word. It seemed to be a day for exciting secrets!

'Hugh Trevanson's got hold of a lorry,' he explained as we drove home, 'and we're trying to make a carnival float the kids can be on. Can we use your raft?'

'Of course!' I agreed eagerly. 'What sort of float, Dad?'

'South Sea Island. We can get the kids in brown tights and vests, cover any remaining white bits with brown body-make-up, put them in sarongs, and make "thrones" for them, using lots of pampas grass and flowers. Stella and Podge are being beautified tomorrow afternoon, so we'll cast Stella as the Great White Queen – she can wear that fancy gear of hers – and Podge can be a tourist or a missionary.'

'A missionary!' I decided. 'Preferably in a cooking pot!'

'If we can make or borrow one,' Dad agreed. 'We'll drape some fishing nets around, have yellow crepe paper for sand, and your raft. Andy, Dave, Podge and Jane can do all the moving – I've suggested Andy and Dave do some kind of war dance. John's going to be taking photos.'

'What about me?' I asked, though I could guess the answer. 'Aren't I allowed to ride on the lorry?'

'Sorry,' Dad said gently. 'No. You might forget your back and join in the dancing, or jump off.'

I was a bit disappointed, but I accepted it without protest. After all, what really mattered was that the kids would have a chance to shine. I'd had my bit of glory. On Saturday, I'd just have to sit back and clap everyone else.

'It's a surprise for them,' Mum explained. 'And because I need your help making costumes and paper flowers, the kids have been led to believe you're going to hospital tomorrow and Friday as a day-patient.'

I almost moaned then, because on the Friday a friend of Mr Kersey's who had his own plane was taking them to an air show, and I'd have loved to go. But just in time I remembered there'd be plenty of chances for me to see air shows, but Burt, Anna and Stella might never get a chance to go in a carnival parade again. So I only said:

'OK, Mum, I promise not to breathe a word of what we're up to.'

I started to make paper flowers that evening. There are lots of real ones around, but Mum hates to see them picked to wilt and die. She supplied me with boxes of tissues and despite help from one of the cats, I got twenty done before I went to bed.

On Thursday morning, Mrs Kersey went into Truro and came back with lots of cheap material for native sarongs. Jane's aunt came over and the three of us made tunics that left one shoulder bare for the girls, and shorts for the boys. I did the sarong tunics which were easier, while Mum and Miss Franklin did the shorts. To be honest, I felt a bit left out of their conversation, because they were both involved with village ladies' things to do with the Carnival and Regatta.

'Can't I do something useful?' I pleaded. 'Even make sandwiches?'

But Mum shook her head. 'You're to take it easy, and that's that,' she insisted.

'I'm not used to doing nothing,' I protested. (Truthfully – I didn't usually get the chance anyway!) But I know when arguing's going to get me nowhere, so I subsided. By lunchtime, we'd finished most of the sewing, and when Dad came home, he said I could go over to St Ives with him, if I liked. He had a friend there who'd produced a pantomime on the lines of Robinson Crusoe and had loads of body-make-up left over.

'It's pretty expensive stuff, so we're lucky to get this lot for free,' he explained.

It occurred to me that we could have problems if – help! – it rained, but Dad and the others had even thought of that. There were upright posts on the corners of the lorry trailer and angle-iron connecting them, so the men were going to rig-up a polythene 'roof'.

'Everything taken care of,' Dad said proudly. I grinned.

'There's just one thing,' I said. 'Does it have to be an absolute, total secret? I think Stella would love to be involved – to feel she'd done something, instead of just sat there. Couldn't she help paint a desert island backdrop to go against the cab?'

Dad looked thoughtful.

'Could she paint something that big?' he asked. I suggested she could do it in bits – tropical birds, monkeys, things like that. If she did them on separate sheets of ordinary paper, the other kids wouldn't guess what they were for. Then they could be stuck together on bright-coloured paper or fabric.

'We can but try,' Dad agreed, and promised to have a word with Mr Kersey, and let Stella into the secret.

Dad had promised to call on his friend at 3.30 p.m. so I made a few more flowers and chatted to Mum as we waited to go. Mum had promised to take Stella and Podge to Truro, mainly to get their hair styled, but also to see the beautician to learn about light make-up.

'Pity Podge isn't going to the dance tonight,' I said. 'The timing would have been just right.'

Mum smiled mysteriously.

'Don't be so sure she won't go,' she said, then changed the subject.

'I thought you'd like to know one really good thing that came out of what happened on Tuesday – though you mustn't talk about it. Carolyn's Mum and Dad have made it up.'

Although I can't really like Carolyn, I did feel pleased for her and Peter. It must be awful thinking your parents are going to divorce. But I couldn't really understand how my rescuing Kevin could have helped!

'Someone rang Carolyn's Mum to tell her the Mirror had been found, and about the rescue,' Mum explained. It still didn't make much sense. I knew Carolyn's mum had been at her office – she's some sort of female executive, and I think the man I saw her with works in the same firm. And her Dad runs his own business, a yacht brokerage, which was why he'd been around to help search for the Mirror. But . . .?

'Her mother got this garbled message about the Mirror being found and a child nearly drowning. She thought it must be Peter or Carolyn, so she raced to the hospital, poor woman. Luckily I was still in Outpatients, waiting for you, when she arrived. I managed to calm her down and tell her what had really happened.'

I could believe it. Mum's awfully good with other people and their problems.

Mum suddenly gave a little shriek of horror, and our conversation ended. Scrap, our youngest cat, had just brought in a rat half as big as he was. And he obviously hadn't killed it – that rat had been a long time dead! But he didn't want to drop it. Dad had to come to the rescue, because I couldn't chase and rugger-tackle a cat now! Soon the ripe corpse was in a plastic bag for Andy's owl. He was trying to teach it to hunt, dragging dead mice and things as lures. Then Podge and Stella had arrived with Mrs Helpman from the WI who was driving them and Mum into Truro. We saw them off, then Dad and I got into our old banger, delivered the rat to the vicarage (Mrs MacKay wasn't too delighted!)

and drove over to St Ives.

Dad's theatrical friend was great fun. He'd been a professional once, and while he and Dad chatted, I was able to look through his scrapbooks of press cuttings and photos. As I looked at them I thought about my daring escapade. Headlines flashed through my mind – 'Local girl saves drowning boy', 'How to be a heroine without really trying' – 'It's a miracle'?

CHAPTER 9

WHO IS SERENA?

When we got back at around 5.15, Mum was ironing an evening dress, and singing as she worked.

'Cinderella shall go to the ball!' she proclaimed. 'Have your dinner, then Andy's coming to take you over to Serena's with this and the carrier bag in the hall.'

I saw the borrowed Red Cross wheelchair in the hall, too, and shuddered.

'Not in *that*!' I began to protest. Then I did a quick double-take.

'Serena?' I asked, 'Who the heck's Serena?'

'Have you called her Podge for so long you've forgotten she has a lovely name?' Mum teased. Then she added seriously, 'Now I don't want you making fun of her on this, because I think it matters a lot to her. Almost as much as sailing!'

'All caterpillars want to turn into butterflies sooner or later,' Dad agreed, taking the make-up into the kitchen. 'Your food's on the table.'

I was still a bit baffled as I sat down to my cheese and egg salad, but Dad filled me in between mouthfuls of lettuce.

'Parents see more than you kids sometimes suspect,' he said. 'And Podge's Mum knew quite a bit about this dance business. And about how Podge felt. So she and your Mum got together.'

He paused, looking for the right words.

'You see, Podge is that bit older than you. She's still the same in a lot of ways, but there's a pretty, feminine young lady trying to break through the tomboy shell. All the girls in her year at school are already interested in clothes, make-up and dancing, and put great importance on having boyfriends. . .'

'Mind you,' Mum called from the kitchen, 'I don't think it's a good thing, but it's boosted by all these silly teenage picture-romance magazines they read. They can't wait to run in a kind of emotional rat-race . . .'

She was on her soap-box again, but Dad cut her short.

'However, we both feel some of it is right and natural. A girl should change into a young lady. And poor Podge has increasingly felt the left-out one, the big joke. She's played along, pretending she doesn't care. But inside it hurts – she'd love to shine, and not just in sailing and swimming. After all, in eighteen months she'll be legally old enough to marry with her parents' consent, and in just over three years she'll be a full adult in the eyes of the Government. Her life can't centre round a muddy creek forever. Even if she goes into top-class sailing, there'll be a social life.'

Now Dad was on *his* soap-box. Given half a chance, parents do waffle on!

'Age is just a measure for convenience,' I interrupted grandly. In two years of Junior Debating Society, I've learned the knack of impressive phrases. 'I shall go on doing what I enjoy whether or not people think it's appropriate to my age!'

'And you,' Dad admitted ruefully, 'will probably get away with it. But Podge can't and she doesn't want to. Now eat up your jelly – Andy said he'd be here at six.'

Just then Andy arrived. He thanked Dad for the rat.

'I've been feeding Fred with mince and pet food mixes, plus hair combed from the cats,' he explained. 'I don't want him to forget what he's supposed to be hunting when he recovers. I think he must have been a pet – he's incredibly daft, and so tame you'd think I'd hatched him!'

I would have liked to go round and see the owl, but there wasn't time. Clutching the dress in a long plastic bag, and the carrier in my lap, I sat nervously in the wheelchair as Andy pushed me down the road.

'What about your secret?' I asked, the minute we were out of earshot of the house. He grinned.

'Sorry, still a secret,' he said, the rotten beast. 'But – do you have to race, or would you mind just sailing, helping with beginners? And would you mind helping to strip down and paint a couple of dinghies during the winter?'

Intensely curious, I admitted I enjoyed any old kind of sailing – Podge was the real racing fanatic, and I hoped she could take my place crewing for Mr Mason so he still had a chance of the cup. But I was quite content to crew and help, though I didn't think I was good enough to teach. And I enjoy scraping and cleaning and painting boats – it's so nice when you stand back and look at this gleaming, gorgeous dinghy that was a scruffy old hulk when you began!

'Good,' Andy said, but he wouldn't give a single thing away, no matter how much I fished. All he would do was promise to tell me all the details as soon as he could.

'Now what's this about a dress for Podge?' he asked.

'Don't know, exactly,' I admitted, 'but I gather she's going to the dance after all. It's all very mysterious. Mum seems to think Podge has this secret yearning to be romantic and feminine and gorgeous.'

Then I remembered I wasn't supposed to make a joke about it, and felt rather ashamed. 'Perhaps she'll tell us when we take the dress round,' I said.

Andy grinned. 'Oh, I'm not coming in!' he said. 'I'm under instructions that this is Girls Only.'

So when he'd pushed me there – on the back wheels for the last bit, the bumpy farm lane – he deposited me at the house and went to play with the pups. Podge's Mum took me into the living room. Podge was there with Stella – and wow!

I wolf-whistled, and I was only half kidding. That beautician knew her stuff! I'd always thought of make-up as a load of gunge all over your face, mascara, eye-shadow and what have you. But Podge just had a bit of lipstick, very natural, shaping her mouth. And something on her nose, hiding the sunburned bit. Her face hadn't changed, except her eyebrows had been tidied up, but her hair had been cut and styled to frame it somehow. Of course, she had a nice golden tan and – let's put it this way – from the neck up, she was definitely Serena! Stella looked good, too. The hospital had never done anything with her hair except wash it and keep it tidily short. But it was a lovely colour and the hairdresser had cut it so it looked almost like a pixie cap on Stella's little pixie face.

'You two look fantastic!' I said. Stella smiled, but Podge looked at me closely to make sure I wasn't kidding. Then she smiled too.

'Your Mum's super,' she told me, taking the dress. Mum had only worn it once. It was a pretty apricot silky thing, with short pleated sleeves, a fitted bodice and a skirt that fell straight down in tiny pleats from under the bust. And it fitted nicely.

'Lovely!' Stella approved.

It's funny. Podge has been my best friend – girl friend that is – for ages, but when I looked at her all dressed up, I felt I was looking at a stranger. It was a curiously lonely feeling. Because, even though she was fat, my friend Podge was suddenly rather beautiful; she was Serena and I was frightened I didn't know her any more. I was glad for her – she danced to look at herself in the hall mirror, and danced back with joy in her eyes – but part of me wanted to beg her to go on swimming in the creek, and playing games, and loving sailing. Not to grow up overnight and leave me far behind. And I think I was even a bit jealous!

But I only told her she looked smashing. So did Stella, who was wearing the disco thing she'd bought in Falmouth. But I knew in my heart it was different for Stella. No matter how much she was made to look pretty and dressed up, she was still stuck in her chair; she couldn't whirl round the dance floor, or even do her own hair. But she was concerned only for Podge.

'Now you can go to the dance!' she said happily, and I squeezed her hand.

'One day,' I promised, 'you'll leave that hospital and go to parties and dances, and a super boy will fall madly in love with you.'

I only said it to give her a dream, but as the words came out they turned into a promise in my heart.

Podge didn't hear. She ran off, and came back a minute later with a dress.

'This is for your Mum, a swap for hers,' she said. 'She told me she could make it into something for herself.'

Then it all came out, and I understood at last. Podge had chosen a very pretty pattern, but the picture on the pattern showed the dress on a tall, willowy girl and the same dress on Podge looked like ... Well, have you seen those pudgy, frilly fairy dolls? Yuk! That was why Podge had told Alan she couldn't go. Then Angela, the beast, had seen her that same evening in the village and added insult to injury by telling her that Alan had asked her, anyway. And that he'd only wanted Podge to help in the kitchens. No wonder she hadn't wanted to talk about it.

'I felt fat and ugly and awful,' Podge admitted, remembering it. 'But your Mum convinced me I wasn't. I didn't want to go to the dance, but Mum and Dad said they'd take me, and your Mum told me the brave thing would be to go there and face the challenge and show them they hadn't hurt me or made me miserable — show them I wasn't a big, fat joke but a . . .'

'A pretty girl!' Stella finished triumphantly. 'And you are!'

'I felt I had to be brave,' Podge continued softly, looking at me, 'because you'd been so brave. I decided I'd never run away from a challenge either . . .'

Honestly, I felt a fraud and a creep, but what could I say? Except the truth.

'You're braver than me,' I assured her, 'and you look just great. You'll knock them sideways tonight.'

'I'm going too,' Stella said eagerly, 'just to watch the first bit. I love dances!'

I thought about Mum, who loved dances too. But Dad could hardly ever afford to take her. And now, cheerfully and casually, she'd 'swopped' her one and only decent evening dress for an awful thing she'd never have time to alter. Just to make Podge happy! I didn't think I'd have been so big-hearted. I'd have looked for something second-best that didn't matter.

But Mum was a Christian. Suddenly I wanted to be more like Mum. At least I could begin in a small way.

'Podge,' I said, then remembered, 'I mean, Serena,

would you like to borrow my gold dove pendant? It'd look smashing with that dress.'

'Yes, please.'

'I'll run and get it!' I promised, then groaned, because of course I wasn't even allowed to walk fast!

'If Andy takes me back now, I'll have time to find it, and you can pick it up on your way to the dance,' I decided. 'And I've got a silver necklace that'd go with your gear, Stella.'

Might as well be really generous and lend my two most super things while I was at it!

'I'll get Andy,' Podge said, running to the door. Stella and I yelled together, 'You mustn't go across the farmyard in that dress!'

So Podge's Mum called Andy, and when he came, he wolf-whistled too.

'Look great, don't they?' I agreed. Then I explained how I wanted to get straight home to find the jewellery.

'I'll run,' he offered and I shuddered.

'Not pushing me in that rotten chair, you won't,' I assured him. 'I feel downright unsafe in it as it is! Even us heroines have our limits! Stella, I reckon you deserve the Victoria Cross for every time we've pushed you in yours!'

So we went home at a sensible sort of speed; it was a bit uphill anyway, and I helped, turning the wheels as Andy pushed. Half way, we stopped for a breather. It was a beautiful evening, the late sun glinting on the creek — a good to be alive evening.

And just like that, I knew. I wasn't fighting any more. I didn't hear him knock, I just knew I could open the door and he'd be there. Jesus, I mean. Podge had said I wouldn't run away from a challenge — Jesus was a challenge, and I had been running. But not any more.

'Andy,' I said simply, 'It's happened. I don't quite

114

know why now but I finally do want Jesus with all my heart.'

It didn't even matter that it sounded corny.

'Great! Fran, that's fantastic!'

Andy crouched by the chair to be on my level, and I've never seen him look quite so happy – he looked like I felt! Then he hugged me.

'Should I ... well, say or do anything special?' I asked, with visions of people marching down to an altar to Declare Themselves for Christ. Andy shook his head.

'You don't have to,' he said. 'It's what's inside that matters. But you could pray – just talk to Jesus.'

I thought I might feel silly but all of a sudden it was quite easy just to talk to Jesus as though he was standing next to me. I said sorry for fighting him for so long; then thanked him for things he'd done, all the help he'd given me, and for taking me on. And I asked him to help me stay in there with him, to serve him and help other people.

Anyway – after that, we were quiet for a bit, too happy for words. I felt warm and peaceful and loved. Neither of us spoke until we reached my house, then I said, 'Mum and Dad will be thrilled!'

Andy nodded. He gave my arm a squeeze, then left me at the door. I think he knew this was something special for me to share with them, and tactfully vanished.

Mum was cooking and Dad was reading, both in the kitchen. I sneaked unnoticed to my room, got the two necklaces, then came down and stood in the doorway.

'Podge and Stella looked fantastic,' I said, 'now stand by for an important announcement!'

They turned, smiling, wondering what I was up to now.

'I'm a Christian,' I told them. 'As we were coming

back from Podge's place, I made up my mind.'

Mum ran across and hugged me, despite her floury hands.

Dad, as usual, was more restrained.

'Good,' he said, smiling. 'Does Andy know?'

'Yes. He's dead chuffed.'

Then Podge rang the doorbell. I did the necklace up for her, and she twirled to show Mum and Dad how good she looked in Mum's dress. Half nervous, half excited, she burbled her thanks to Mum, promised to tell me all about the dance the next day, took the other necklace for Stella, and ran.

'I do hope she has a good time!' I said.

Dad grinned. 'People like Podge,' he assured me. 'And she looks lovely. Don't worry – they'll ask her to dance.'

'Well, I'm going to bed. It's been quite a day – quite a week, really!' I said, yawning.

And as I climbed the stairs I knew my friendship with Andy would be extra-special now, and I knew we were a family in a way we had never quite been before. I was bubbling with happiness, but not too excited to fall asleep the moment my head touched the pillow.

CHAPTER 10

DREAMS COME TRUE

On Friday morning, I had to go to the hospital for X-rays. They were good – the consultant had a look and said my spine was already beginning to straighten itself out, so the twisting was a result of the accident, not something nasty that would need treatment.

To my relief, Mum also took back the Red Cross wheelchair!

That morning I had an unexpected visit from Sarah. She'd had a go at the Corsairs about the disabled children, and they had decided unanimously to make the kids Honorary Corsairs.

'We thought they might like to have our burgees to fix to their wheelchairs,' she said, 'and we'd send them the Corsair News – a letter every month about what we'd done and anything we'd won.'

I thought that was a really nice idea, and told her so.

'Even Carolyn agreed,' she said, 'though she and Peter won't be Corsairs much longer. Their Dad's got himself a cruiser and the whole family's going to sail together in that, at weekends. They're flogging the Mirror to the vicar after the Regatta.'

To the *vicar*? For Andy? Perhaps that was the secret he couldn't quite tell me! I couldn't ask him, though, because he was off with the kids.

Podge wasn't. She'd been practising swimming and

diving all morning, and came to us for lunch. And actually refused ice-cream!

'I'm dieting,' she explained, with an embarrassed grin. 'Daffy, it was super last night! I danced nearly every dance. Even Alan asked me twice! But better still, Hugh asked me lots and lots of times.'

That was something. Hugh's sixteen and already a top class sailor. Normally he doesn't notice us lesser beings.

Podge rattled on joyfully about what people had worn, who'd been there, the dances and spot prizes, how the Commodore of the Sailing Club had waltzed Stella round in her chair and the Chairman of the Parish Council had danced with her in the Gay Gordons, of all things!

'Three girls from my form were there,' she ended triumphantly, 'and they couldn't believe it when they saw me! Now I'm going to try to get down to a size 10 — then they'll really have to watch out!'

She grinned as she spoke, half-joking, but I knew she was looking into a golden future when she'd not be Podge any more, but slender, lovely, popular Serena. And I hoped it would come true. In fact, I felt sure it would — for this week, at least, life was touched with a glorious magic guaranteed to give happy endings!

In the afternoon, I made yet more paper flowers, and helped Mum tie them to fishing nets (scrounged off one of Mr Kersey's fishing friends) and to the fake grass we'd got to cover the kids' 'thrones' (scrounged off one of Dad's friends who has a fruit and veg. stall in Truro market). The lorry was parked under Podge's Dad's big barn and in the evening several of the men finished decorating it, and put my raft in position. It looked terrific! There were floats being worked on in a lot of barns and backyards, and the bunting was up on the streets and all round the playing field. The whole village hummed with Carnival activity. In the village hall, girls were competing for Regatta Queen and Carnival Queen (they always leave it to the last minute). They always have to be local, and more than just pretty – the Regatta one has to be good at some water sport, and the Carnival one has usually done something special for the village, raised lots of money for charity, something like that.

All my friends were off having last-minute practices or polishing their boats or whatever, so I went up to my room to write. But I hadn't been there more than ten minutes when Andy arrived. So I came down again, made milk shakes, and we sat in the kitchen.

'Is your Dad buying you a Mirror?' I demanded, and he laughed.

'Word gets round fast! Would you believe a Mirror and two Celtics? But for the Crusaders, not for me!'

I knew about the Crusaders, though I'd never been to them. They were a holiday club for kids, run by people from a group of local churches. For two days each week during the summer holidays they offered activities to any local or holiday-makers' kids who wanted to come. They did things like orienteering, nature study, drama and pony trekking – anything they could afford to do or get free instructors for, really.

'Is this your secret?' I asked, and he nodded.

'Only it needn't be a secret any more – it's finally confirmed and decided. Dad was at a meeting last night. They've been thinking of adding water sport of some kind for a while, but the cost was too great. Now somebody's given them a grant and because of what happened to Kevin, and the way you were able to rescue him, Dad's managed to persuade them that sailing, with an emphasis on water safety and a bit of life saving thrown in, would be a very good idea.'

'And . . .' He paused, looking at me, making sure I knew something even better was coming but determined to keep me in suspense, until I wanted to thump him! Then it came out in a rush . . .

'And guess who have been suggested for Boatswains, to do the boats up and look after them? And Able Crew to help with the beginners?'

'Us?'

'Us!'

I could just imagine it. We'd both be fit as fiddles by next summer, and we'd have the fun of working on the boats during the winter too. It'd be tremendous experience, helping kids to learn sailing, and it would mean while I was with the Crusaders, Podge could have my Mirror. Best of all, it would mean two lots of sailing kids on the creek – Corsairs *and* Crusaders! We could have contests!

'Yippee!' I yelled, and but for my back, I would have done a dance of triumph there and then. Then I had an Awful Thought.

'I've only got my RYA Elementary,' I admitted. 'I don't know if that's good enough for helping with beginners.'

'There'll be trained instructors as well,' Andy explained. 'We'll be mainly used for demonstrating things, and being crew when a beginner takes a boat out by themselves the first time. Anyway – the Crusaders committee has agreed to cough up to send us on the Youth Service Training week in the Spring over at St Just, to get our Intermediates.'

I sat there, sipping my milk shake. 'I'm going to wake up soon,' I muttered. 'So many fantastic things are happening, this has got to be a dream.'

'Shall I pinch you?' Andy offered helpfully — but I wriggled away before he could! Then we both got down to discussing ideas. Maybe we could even link in the Crusaders with the disabled kids, somehow.

Saturday, Regatta and Carnival day, dawned bright and clear. At first there was only a very light wind, then it stiffened and by 9 a.m. was a perfect Force 4. There was a tremendously festive air over all the village. As well as the official bunting, lots of people had put up their own flags and decorations.

Poor Dad hadn't been able to get anyone to look after his shop until lunchtime, so he would miss the morning races. But for the rest of us, it was all go. Suddenly, everyone was organizing everyone else. The minibus turned up with the kids, who were to watch the Regatta from Mr Trevanson's shop, and I piled in with them. Stella winked at me, and I winked back. I did have one horrible thought — what if the kids didn't want to be natives on a float? But from what they were saying and what Dave was translating when the rest of us couldn't understand, Anna and Burt were both really envious of people taking part, and longed to join in, so that was all right.

The plan was for us to watch the morning events, have a picnic lunch, and stay until the Regatta and water sports finished in the early afternoon. We'd skip the raft race, tell the kids about the float, and get them ready to be in the procession at 5 p.m. Make-up and costumes would be done at the Kerseys.

It was a good thing the Regatta was really exciting, or I'm sure I'd have let the cat out of the bag. But I was soon engrossed in the racing. I was rooting for Podge in the Mirror class and Junior handicap, and was delighted to see her beat Carolyn by a mile; but I also cheered

Sarah when she won the Topper class. But Hugh had entered the handicap class with his Laser, so nobody else stood a chance – he even came third in the Laser class against really experienced men.

Lunch passed in a haze of bubbling happiness. The kids were really glowing, and people kept on coming up to congratulate me on my life saving, many of them people I didn't even know by name. Mr Trevanson said it was because there'd been an article in *The West Briton,* and perhaps I should start selling autographs!

After lunch, clouds came over and we all feared a wash-out – but they passed, and it was really warm for the water sports. Dave won the diving but Podge came a close second and she won the Ladies' Distance Medley although most of the other competitors were much older than her.

Mum signalled me at 2.30, and I saw Mr Kersey speaking to the kids as I went to her. I heard their cries of delight and Stella's joyful laughter as they learned about the float. In fact, I hardly took in what Mum was saying at first, because I was listening to them. Then I registered that she was saying it was time for *me* to go home and change.

'You mean, I'm going on the float after all?' I yelled, and she smiled mysteriously.

'You're going in the parade – you'll see how, when we get home,' was all she'd say. And although it took us a good fifteen minutes to get there at my snail's pace, she absolutely refused to give the least hint of what she meant. And I didn't guess, though I imagined – with my reputation for playing the fool – that I was probably going to be one of the people in daft fancy dress who collect for charity from the crowds along the carnival route.

But it wasn't a silly costume waiting for me on my

bed. It was a long dress, the most beautiful long dress imaginable, in aquamarine silky fabric. On top of it was a little silver crown. Then I understood. I still couldn't believe, but I knew what was happening. The Carnival Queen has to have attendants, and the attendants are always local schoolgirls who've done something special. This year, Sue Harris, who'd won a Duke of Edinburgh award even though she's deaf, was to be one, and sixteen-year-old Liz Penaluna, who's just been chosen to compete for England in some girls' cross-country, was another. But me?

'They can't mean it!' I gasped, and Mum hugged me.

'They do,' she insisted. 'Now I'm going to run a bath for you, then Sheila's coming in to do your hair. Wash it in the bath.'

In a dream, I obeyed. Sheila's one of Mum's friends, and a good amateur hairdresser. When she'd finished with me, my long fly-away hair was coiled up beautifully and studded with tiny flowers. Talcummed and perfumed, I stepped into the dress and it fitted perfectly (don't ask me how, I suppose they checked one of my ordinary ones). There were little silver heeled shoes and gloves to go with it. Then the crown was put on my head, and I stared in the mirror at a girl I'd never seen before. Someone quite grown-up and almost beautiful.

'Mum?' I whispered, scared.

She said softly, 'You look lovely.'

'Jesus?' I prayed, but silently this time. 'Thank you! I'll try not to get too big-headed, honest.' And it was almost as though even he was happy, happy with and for me, watching me enjoy his glorious gift of life.

Then I kissed Mum and started to cry for pure happiness. She dabbed the tears away.

'No red, spotty face!' she teased. 'But I know how

you feel. I could almost cry too, I'm so proud! Dad's back – he'll be in the crowd waiting to take your picture as you drive by, so remember to give him a royal wave!'

'Have we time to show my dress to the kids and see their float before I go on mine?' I asked, with a final sniff. Mum glanced at her watch and agreed.

'But not walking. Not in that dress,' she said firmly; and went next door, to return with Sheila. We went down to Podge's farm in Sheila's car, and the float was in the yard ready to start. The kids were smiling so broadly, I thought their faces would split, while Andy and Dave were practising a war dance and ferocious yells. Podge was standing in this great iron pot (well, crepe paper and cardboard actually), a cannibal lunch. Andy saw me first and whistled – the others just gawped at me like stranded fish. I was a bit afraid Podge might think I was trying to steal her thunder – after she'd looked so gorgeous on Thursday night and I'd said I didn't care what I looked like, and everything – but she seemed really pleased.

'You look super,' she told me. 'Quite majestic!'

'We'd better not call her Daffy any more,' Andy teased, 'just "Your Highness".'

Then we were all laughing and admiring each other, and I saw Stella's paintings, a proud blaze of colour against the back of the cab.

'You're sure to win a prize!' I crowed, then Mum looked at her watch and ordered me back into the car. We drove down to the playing field, where the parade was to start and finish. There were several floats, walkers and riders in fancy dress already there, and the Carnival Queen was on a really sumptuous one, with a gold throne on a purple velvet dias. I recognized her – Barbara Poldhu. She teaches at the village school, runs the Cubs and is engaged to a local farmer. Her dress was white, really beautiful lace with a scarlet sash. She waved to me, and a man literally carried me across the field and lifted me up onto the float so I couldn't get my shoes or hem mucky. The other two girls arrived five minutes later and we talked a bit, shyly, too excited to say much. My seat wasn't very comfortable, but I was far too thrilled to even notice my aching back. One of the Carnival officials came along and gave us baskets of sweets — our job was to throw these to children in the crowd.

Soon the field was full up, with bands and majorettes coming in and practising. I saw judges start going down the line of floats, and hoped the kids would get a rosette. Then we had to smile for photographs, and the whole procession began to move off very slowly.

It was almost like a coronation. We proceeded through the village, waving and throwing sweets. All the children lining the route were wide-eyed with excitement, especially the littlest ones. Adults were smiling, too, and though there were policemen around, they didn't have to do anything except stop boys on skateboards from getting in the way of the lorries. Our Regatta and Carnival is always so good that people come from neighbouring villages, even sometimes from Truro and Falmouth, to compete in it or watch; and this year there seemed to be more than ever. I suppose it took us three-quarters of an hour to get back to the playing-fields, but it seemed like minutes and I would gladly have gone round again!

However, that was the end. The Carnival Queen had to go home and change yet again for the evening open-air dancing, and I had to go to the Kerseys, where we were all having our farewell tea with the kids. Carefully holding my skirt, I walked over to the kids' float and there, stuck to the cab, was a red First Prize rosette.

'Another great White Queen has come,' Andy said, bowing low to Stella. 'May we invite her aboard, Your Majesty?'

I nearly told him, with regal dignity, to get knotted; but Stella smiled.

'Pray join us, O Foreign Queen,' she acknowledged, and Mr Kersey hoisted me aboard. I travelled back with them, talking ten to the dozen and getting bits of brown body-make-up on my dress; but it was mine to keep, and washable, so that didn't matter.

It was easier to have tea dressed up, Mrs Kersey decided, and then Podge, Dave, Andy, Jane and I could change and clean up in our own homes while with Miss Franklin's help, the Kerseys cleaned up the kids. John wasn't there – he'd wanted to go home and develop the film he'd taken, so the kids could have photographs to take back to the hospital with them when they left in the morning.

So assorted natives, missionary, and two White Queens had a Chinese take-away meal by popular vote (decided earlier when I wasn't there, but I didn't mind, I love Chinese food). Afterwards, we had a sing-song, and finished with Old Lang Syne. I'm not ashamed to say that all us girls burst into tears. Burt was also crying, the tears streaming down his twisted face.

'You'll come back,' we promised, 'and we'll write.'

I gave my little silvery crown to Stella as a souvenir, and my story. She gave me her bird of paradise painting. Then I hugged her, said goodbye, and walked home with Podge, Jane and Andy. We were all sniffing. We could hear the first music of the evening drifting up from the playing fields, but we just felt empty and a bit sad. At the main road we split up and went our different ways. The glorious day was over, and early tomorrow, the kids would go home.

But I knew it wasn't the end – only the beginning. The kids would come down again – if faith and love and hope were enough, we'd make it happen! We'd have all kinds of fund-raising, there'd be the link scheme, and in the meantime, Andy and I would have the Crusaders' boats to do up, and a sailing course to look forward to in the Spring. Podge would get slim and beautiful, and I'd remember to call her Serena. Even I might, just might, start tidying myself up a bit! And tomorrow was church. And in all the tomorrows for the rest of my life, there would be Jesus.

My dreams stretched before me in golden promise, and as I walked up the garden path, I was singing.